I0452676

CONTENT ADVISORY

This novel includes depictions of:
- Violence and injury
- Psychological trauma and panic episodes
- Abusive family dynamics
- Supernatural horror elements
- Blood, gore, and body transformation
- Death of characters

Reader discretion is advised.

For my family, by blood or by choice—you taught me what love and survival really mean.

For Charlie, who sat with me through sleepless nights and endless edits.

You remind me time and time again that home isn't a place, its a person.

For Sean and Marina, who inspired me and believed in this story even when I didn't.

And for the dreamers who stay up too late, chasing stars.

This book is proof it's worth it.

"Love, let's talk about love—Is it everything and everything you hoped for? Or do the feeling haunt you?"
~Kendrick Lamar & SZA, "All the Stars"

CHAPTER ONE

ERIN

The problem with Hollywood isn't the monsters in front of the cameras—it's the ones behind them.

My heels click across the rooftop, the sunset burning the LA skyline gold. The wind teases loose strands of hair across my face as I lean on the edge of the balcony, breathing in smog and desperation.

Down below, the world prepares for the red carpet event I'm contractually obligated to attend. Up here, I can pretend for five more minutes that I'm just a girl with a view.

My phone buzzes. I don't look at the screen. I don't need to. I already know who it is.

I answer anyway.

"What, Claudia?"

"Don't sound so surprised," my sister purrs. "It's a big night for you. I'd hate for you to forget where you came from."

I roll my eyes. "You called just to gloat?"

"To remind you," she says. "That you owe everything to me—your role. Your platform. Even the dress you're wearing."

My fingers curl tighter around the iron railing. Cold metal bites into my palm.

"And here I thought you were calling out of sisterly concern."

Her laugh is grating. "Try not to embarrass us out there, Erin. Some of us still have reputations to protect."

The line goes dead.

I stare at the screen until it fades to black, then shove the phone into my clutch with a little more force than necessary. My hand drifts up to my ear before I can stop it—fingers tracing the scar just behind the lobe, where a jagged strip of skin never quite healed right. A reminder. One of many.

The memory unfurls before I can stop it. I'm thirteen again, wearing a dress that cost more than most people's rent, standing alone at the edge of the Immortal Council's winter gala. My first "official" appearance. The marble floor gleams too bright under the chandeliers, making me dizzy.

"Half-breed," comes the whisper—not bothering to be quiet enough that I won't hear. I turn to see Elder Monroe's wife, her diamond earrings catching the light as she leans toward her companion. "Fae and vampire. Disgusting combination." My fairy wine flute nearly slips from my fingers.

A pure-blood Elder saunters past, his gaze sliding over me as if I were invisible—the same man who'd spent twenty minutes fawning over Claudia moments before. My hands tremble, and I notice the shadows beneath the buffet table darkening, responding to my distress. Even then, my powers betrayed me when I was upset. The shadows pool around my feet—the only allies in a ballroom full of immortals who'd spent centuries despising me for what my parents had done.

That night, I learned what I was: a political inconvenience, tolerated only because of my father's influence. Not vampire enough. Not fae enough. Not anything enough. I rub the rough patch slowly, grounding myself. The old pain flickers like static.

My reflection stares back at me from the sliding glass door when I turn around, distorted slightly by the tinted glass.

Polished. Poised. Pretend.

The dress clings in all the right ways; my makeup is flawless, my smile just sweet enough to keep people guessing. But the longer I look, the more I see her.

My mother.

Same bone structure. Same eyes. Same grief hidden behind a practiced smile.

Is this how she felt?

Back when she was playing their game—schmoozing the elites of Hollywood's immortal society, pretending it didn't cost her everything.

I swallow hard.

Claudia doesn't usually demand my presence unless it's about appearances... or leverage.

A chill creeps down my spine.

Is this about the annual mentorship program?

The mortal-immortal PR farce the Council parades out every year. I hope not, but I get a bad feeling. I don't get to say no. Not when I have a brand to maintain and secrets to keep.

I let go of the scar. Smooth my hair. Fix my smile.

Then I step through the door and head for the elevator.

Time to play nice.

***

The car ride is short; the silence shorter.

By the time we pull up, the cameras are already flashing like a thousand tiny lightning strikes.

Nathan opens the door with a tired sigh. "You good?"

"As good as I ever am," I mutter, gathering the folds of my gown like armor.

He doesn't smile. He hasn't really, not since we were kids. But his eyes meet mine with a weight that grounds me—solid, steady. Nathan may not say much, but when the world tilts sideways, he's always been the hand that keeps me upright.

"You sure you want to do this?" he asks, voice low.

I want to say no. That I'd rather set myself on fire than walk into a sea of cameras and immortal politics dressed like someone who belongs.

But I just nod.

He offers his arm without another word, and I take it. His grip is firm.

Familiar.

The only real thing in a night built on illusion.

I step out into the lights, and they swallow me whole.

The red carpet is a gauntlet.

Every flashing camera, every pair of watching eyes—it all feels like a spotlight trained on the one person who doesn't belong.

Me.

I adjust the neckline of my borrowed dress and try not to trip over the hem. Nathan said it made me look "ethereal and intimidating," but all I can feel is the weight of all their expectations bearing down on me.

I don't belong in this world of polished teeth and perfect lies, but here I am—being paraded like a show pony for a movie I can barely believe I'm in.

A reporter steps in our path, shoving a mic toward my face. "Erin Cowles! It's your first major red carpet as a lead—how does it feel carrying the family legacy?"

I flinch. It's subtle, but Nathan feels it. His fingers tighten slightly on my arm.

I open my mouth, but—

Claudia materializes beside me, smiling so sharply it could draw blood. "She's honored," she cuts in smoothly. "Our family has always been committed to excellence. Erin is no exception."

My mouth snaps shut. My spine stiffens.

I glance at her out of the corner of my eye. She doesn't even look at me.

"Smile, Erin," Claudia mutters under her breath, still facing the cameras. "You're not just an actress tonight. You're a legacy."

I bite back the reply burning on my tongue.

Legacy. That word is poison when it comes from her lips.

My last name isn't even mine. The Cowles name belongs to a man who barely acknowledged my existence for most of my life—and a family that only remembers I exist when it's convenient for PR.

Nathan shifts again, subtly blocking the next camera flash with his shoulder. His presence doesn't erase the sting, but it softens the edge.

"You look like you're going to stab someone," he says under his breath.

"That's because I might," I mutter.

He huffs, almost a laugh, and steers me past the worst of the press like a seasoned bodyguard instead of my half-brother.

With him around, I don't feel completely exposed. I can handle fake smiles and forced charm if I have one person who doesn't make me feel like a fraud.

Just one.

Inside the venue, chandeliers sparkle overhead like upside-down stars. The room hums with tension as industry giants and immortal royalty mingle, salvation and damnation in the same space. And that's when I realize...

This isn't just a premiere. It's a battlefield.

A waiter threads through the crowd with champagne flutes that frost the moment certain guests touch them. Across the room, a producer laughs too loudly while the vampire beside him stands completely still, her eyes tracking his movements. At the bar, a fae whispers to a mortal actress whose pupils dilate as she tries and fails to look away. The rich and famous mingle, either blind to or deliberately ignoring the supernatural undercurrents.

I hover near the back, neither vampire nor fae enough to fit in. Old vampire houses trade polite nods with fae envoys, hiding grudges behind practiced smiles. The subtle shimmer of glamour magic clings to skin and clothes, smoothing imperfections, heightening allure.

Nathan nudges me. "Brace yourself."

Claire is gliding toward us like she owns the place—blonde hair slicked back, stiletto heels, and a gold dress that screams power.

"Daughter," she says coolly. "Try not to embarrass the family tonight."

I raise a brow. "You mean the family that forgot I existed until a few years ago?"

She doesn't flinch. "The Council is watching. Don't give them a reason to question your place."

"I didn't realize I had one." I muse.

Nathan steps between us before I can say more. "Erin, you promised to meet the director. He's over by the bar."

I let him lead me away. Claire's glare follows.

We don't make it far before a microphone screeches overhead.

I wince. On stage stands a severe-looking woman in a structured blazer, her smile tighter than her bun.

"Attention, esteemed guests," she announces. "The heritage meeting will commence shortly. Please make your way to the designated conference room."

Nathan and I share a look.

Immortals love their meetings.

We follow the flow down a gold-trimmed corridor into a side chamber of velvet chairs and low murmurs. Nathan then guides me through a hidden door and down narrow stairs to the real meeting room. Beneath the glitz, a heavy table seats veteran vampires with their house crests, fae diplomats in simple yet elegant attire, and hybrids like me perched on the edge. Above each seat, a lamp flickers, casting spectral halos that signify the weight of each elder's vote—some beams are luminous, others mere flickers.

At the foot of the stairs, a guard scans me with a silver device. It stings. It always stings, as if it's judging my worth, not just confirming my immortality.

The room quiets as an Elder sits down at the table. Snow-white hair. Bright red eyes. His voice is gruff but smooth with a southern twang.

"Welcome, everyone," he begins. "We're here to discuss the future of our society, and the crucial role we each play in maintaining the balance between our world and the mortal realm."

My mind drifts while they hash out new boundaries in West Hollywood. But I listen in when the topic of new alliances is brought up, all while keeping my expression blank. The centuries-old vampires dominate the discourse with voices that echo authority, their votes illuminating clusters of lights, enough to carve shadows on the polished table surface. In contrast, the younger representatives and the fae, their lights like scattered stars, find their voices carried on subtler currents of influence.

Same discussions. Different year.

I'm halfway to zoning out completely when his tone shifts.

"...We'd usually open the mentorship program to applicants, but this year we have a volunteer."

Murmurs ripple through the crowd. I look up. Claudia rises smoothly.

I blink. *Claudia wouldn't—*

"I am thrilled," Claudia says, rising with perfect poise, "to announce that my dear sister, Erin, has graciously agreed to participate in this year's mentorship program."

Time stops.

My head jerks up. My heart stops. The chamber buzzes with a symphony of discord—some railing against the fusion of worlds, others advocating for evolution amid shifting tides.

No.

She didn't.

She wouldn't.

She did.

My mouth goes dry as all eyes turn to me.

The weight of a hundred immortal stares slams into my chest as I gaze into the crowd.

Claudia smiles, all venom and veneer. "Erin's unique perspective and experience make her the perfect candidate to guide a promising mortal through our world. I have no doubt she will make the Cowles family proud."

My lungs forget how to breathe.

Not again.

My hand curls around the seat's edge, knuckles whitening as memories flood back.

—Elder Marceline's courtyard, five years ago, when Claudia last "volunteered" me. I'd been so eager to please, manipulating shadows into elegant patterns between marble columns while vampires twice my age nodded approval.

"More height on the eastern wall," Marceline had instructed, and I'd complied, stretching darkness into delicate archways. Then came the whispers.

"Clumsy half-breed."

"Not like her sister."

"Cowles in name only."

My concentration fractured. The shadows responded to my panic, writhing like living things, knocking over the centerpiece—a marble cherub that crashed onto the birthday boy's leg. His screams. The shadows lashing out at guests, feeding on my horror. Elder Koenig's face as he pinned me against the wall, fangs bared. The shadows. The screaming. The way no one stepped in until it was too late—until I'd lost control—

I feel the echo of that old pain ripple through me.

Cold. Empty.

But I can't let it show.

I force myself to smile back. The Elder's gaze weighs upon me, nodding in approval. My fingers clutch the chair, a silent battle on the cusp of eruption. I return the grin, a serene facade over roiling chaos.

"Thank you, Claudia," I say smoothly. "I'm honored by your faith in me, and I'll do my best to live up to the Cowles family name."

But my words taste bitter.

I reach for the nearest glass on a passing tray.

Fairy wine. Of course.

I down it in one go.

Let Claudia smile. Let the Council stare.

I'll play their game as always.

***

The moment the Council adjourns, the crowd floods back into the ballroom like nothing happened. I drift through the press of silk and secrets, another glass of fairy wine in my hand and a thousand carefully schooled expressions hiding the churn in my gut. Nathan hovers close. I know he's waiting for me to explode, or implode, or both. But I don't. Not yet. Not when the room is full of predators dressed like patrons.

I weave my way through the throng, the cacophony of chatter and clinking glasses gradually fading as I slip into the refuge of a secluded lounge. The lighting is soft, a stark contrast to the brilliant chaos of the ballroom.

"Erin!" Wren appears like a shot of neon in a sea of monochrome. Her dress is all glitter and mischief, and her lipstick matches the chaos in her eyes. She pulls me into a side-hug, already buzzing with gossip.

"Okay, what the hell was that? Mentorship program? Who forced Claudia into charity work?"

"More like she shoved me headfirst into it," I mutter.

André materializes behind her, tux undone, drink in hand, and wearing the smug grin of someone who has definitely threatened a producer this week.

"Escape artist, are we?" André grins, offering me a bubbling concoction that gleams under the dim light.

"Claudia's just mad you're more interesting than she is," he says, then raises his glass. "To being volunteered for PR deathtraps—may your mentee be hot and legally expendable."

I clink my glass to his then down the drink, savoring the momentary burn.

"Cheers to that." Wren wiggles her eyebrows. "Ooh. Is this one cute? I hope they're cute. If we have to endure this charade, you should at least get a view."

"They'll probably be attractive as usual," I say flatly. "But entirely too mortal."

Nathan mutters, "So basically doomed."

André chuckles, sharing a conspiratorial wink. "Once, I had to mentor a reality TV producer. Ended the night with a cast convinced they were trapped in a haunted mansion."

Before I can answer, a familiar chill crawls down my spine. Lysander enters the room, parting the crowd as he makes his way toward us—silver hair combed back just above his shoulders, suit midnight black and tailored to kill. He smiles like he knows every secret in the room.

"Erin, darling," he purrs, appearing at my elbow. "Roped into the mentorship circus already? How... thrilling."

"Thrilling's one word for it," I say, dry as bone.

He takes my free hand and presses a kiss to my knuckles. His lips are cold. With a graceful flick of his wrist, our glasses frost over, the liquid within twisting into a delicate ice phoenix.

"A token of my admiration," he murmurs, his voice low and velvety.

"Quite the conjurer, aren't you?" I retort, masking the unease curling in my chest.

He leans in, his breath a whisper against my ear. "Be wary of Claudia's intentions. Should you need help navigating murky waters, I've got connections that would make Claudia scream."

"I'll keep that in mind," I say, noticing movement from the door.

And as swiftly as he arrived, he's gone, leaving behind an otherworldly chill. The room darkens as Morana enters the room and floats through the crowd. Her gown shifts like smoke, her eyes a little too sharp to be called elegant. She catches my gaze and smiles, then tilts her head, motioning me over.

Challenge or invitation?

I raise my brow as I make my way over to her at the bar. "Morana. Care to make this night less boring?"

"A game?" she asks, her voice smooth and velvety. "What are the stakes?"

"Drinking. Shot for shot. Last one standing wins a favor—no questions asked."

Her smile widens to absurd proportions, and for a moment, I'm thankful there are no humans present to see.

"You've no idea what you're in for," She signals a server, who appears instantly with two glittering shot glasses of Banshee's Breath. I stare down at the smoking black liquid that shimmers in the glass.

Wren lets out a gasp beside me. "You're drinking that?"

I glance at her and remind myself to keep better track of my surroundings.

"Wish me luck," I murmur, clinking my glass against Morana's. The crowd around us stirs, their curiosity piqued by the rare spectacle.

"To the bold hybrid who dares to challenge a pure-blood," Morana announces, her voice as smooth as silk.

I knock back the Banshee's Breath, gasping for air as it feels like I've just lit my throat on fire.

"My dear, are you sure you're cut out for this?" Morana teases with a twinkle in her eye.

I nod, wiping my mouth with the back of my hand, and meet her eyes with a smile. In response, Morana snaps her fingers, and the server produces a tray full of identical shimmering black shots.

Shit. Round two. Can't quit now.

Instead, I keep it going, matching her shot for shot.

"Aren't hybrids always trying to straddle two worlds?" Morana muses, her words laced with centuries of tradition and the whispers of old grudges.

Smiling through the sting, I reply, "True. But that's why we're survivors."

The rhythmic clink of glasses marks each round, my hybrid physiology allowing me to withstand the fiery onslaught longer than expected. The challenge becomes emblematic of my struggle—an unending quest to carve out a place in a world that considers me an abomination.

At some point, I look over and Wren has vanished. *Good,* I think to myself. *Fewer witnesses for what's about to happen.*

We've just finished our tenth round of shots when I notice. She falters first, just slightly. Her regal calm cracks, and I see her glamor peel back, revealing her true spectral form. She recovers quickly, but her movements betray a slight sluggishness.

"Is this trial proving too much, dear Erin?" she jests, though a hint of respect colors her tone.

I seize the moment with a wink and a final toast as I knock back my eleventh shot. She collapses gracefully as she tries to reach for her shot glass, laughing even as she hits the floor.

"Well played, Erin Cowles," she whispers. "You've earned a favor. But keep this between us."

"Naturally. Our little secret." I hand off my empty glass to a stunned server and drift back toward the dance floor. The Banshee's Breath buzzing in my blood and something close to pride blooms in my chest. The Council can throw whatever it wants at me.

I'll smile. I'll sip. I'll survive. Just like always.

CHAPTER TWO

LIAM

I wasn't born for heat. My mother used to say I was "like a vampire," which became our private joke back in rainy Portland, where I spent childhood summers hiding in the basement with her old film collection instead of at summer camp. So when the director yells "cut!" and I'm standing under a broiling array of warehouse lights, sweat pooling in places that should be physically impossible, I wonder what Mom would say if she could see me now—her theater kid, finally on a real set, albeit melting.

But at least I nail the scene. In the take, I stagger through an alleyway, face bruised and artfully bloodied, and scream at a side character named "Frankie" with enough raw desperation to make the boom operator flinch. I channel Mom's face from the night she got the call about Dad—that same hollow fury. The role is small, the production is so indie it might as well be homemade kimchi, but rent is rent, and I can still taste last week's rejection from a Netflix casting call that would have finally let me send Mom enough money to fix her leaking roof.

"Nice work, Hartley!" shouts Lila, the AD, as she peels gaffer tape from the floor. "If we're lucky, this'll hit six figures on streaming before the bots take over the reviews."

I flash a thumbs-up, trying to ignore the way my shirt adheres to my back. The director, a man who looks like he's been running on

Red Bull and existential dread for three days, nods at me in that way where you're not sure if he's impressed or simply caught in a loop. He reminds me of my acting coach from high school—the one who told me I had the talent but not the connections to make it in this town. Three years later, I'm determined to prove him wrong.

"Break's over in ten, then we reset for the mugging," he calls.

I wipe my face with a grimy towel and drift outside, inhaling the blessedly cool smog. The warehouse lot stretches half a mile from the nearest bodega, hemmed in by a rusted chain-link fence and wild bougainvillea clawing through the gaps. I rest my shoulder against the fence, trying to ignore how my bank account hovers just above zero and how my agent warned me last week that my unpaid parking tickets might get me banned from the lot. Every day feels like a gauntlet—humiliations punctuated by rare chocolate chip cookies from craft services that taste like victory in small bites.

My phone buzzes. I glance at the screen.

Jake.

"Liam! Oh my god, finally," blasts a voice like a sitcom dad on a triple-espresso bender. "I've called twice. You on set?"

I pinch the bridge of my nose. "Hey, Jake," I say, instantly regretting it the second he starts piling on.

"I'm not gonna waste your time. I need you at Eclipse tomorrow morning, sharp. This is it, man. The mentorship program. The one we talked about."

I nearly drop the phone. Cowles is top tier: they groom new actors, get them real auditions, real money.

"Are you screwing with me?"

"Do I sound like a man with the bandwidth for jokes? They want to interview you. And Liam—no sad plaid shirts, okay?"

I glance down at the faded flannel that's become my unofficial uniform.

It's not sad. It's nostalgic.

"I have other shirts," I mumble.

"Good, because if you bomb this, I will personally heckle you on your next set."

"Duly noted," I say. "What's the catch?"

Jake exhales. "No catch. Just be yourself, but, you know, the version of yourself that sounds employable—not the guy who's one existential crisis away from a meltdown. I'll text you the address. Don't be late."

He hangs up without a goodbye. I'm left staring at the screen, heart pounding, until Lila leans out the loading dock door.

"You want back in, or are you waiting for your Oscar now?" she yells, half-laughing, half-teasing.

"Coming!" I shout, but quietly, because the last thing I need is to be that guy who thinks he's too good for background work.

I shove the phone into my pocket and straighten up. The director's pacing, clipboard in hand, ready to film the next take of the mugging gone wrong. I wipe sweat from my jaw and step back onto the set. *Tomorrow*, I tell myself, *I'll dress like I deserve the shot. Tonight, I'll survive this scene.*

***

The next morning, I spend fifteen minutes wrestling my hair into something resembling a haircut and another twenty using YouTube tutorials to fold a pocket square. The result is... acceptable. I look like the best version of myself possible when your entire wardrobe fits in one battered suitcase and half of it's jeans.

I take a deep breath and step into Eclipse's lobby—a cathedral of glass and marble where everyone glides instead of walks. Assistants drift by in perfectly tailored suits, their skin so flawless it's almost eerie. Agents in sky-high heels and loafers float between meetings.

And interns flutter about clutching clipboards as though they're holding the future of cinema itself. At the reception desk, a woman with electric-pink hair and a silver nose ring eyes me over the rim of her laptop. Her once-over is so rapid it might have been a compliment.

"Name?" she asks without looking up.

"Liam Hartley. I'm here for the mentorship interview."

She types with one hand, twirling a pen with the other. "Take a seat, Mr. Hartley. Ms. Cowles will see you at nine."

The waiting area is a masterpiece of controlled chaos—sleek leather chairs, abstract sculptures that look expensive and pointless, and a panoramic wall of glass framing the Hollywood sign like a silent, constant reminder of why we're all here. I settle onto a low leather bench and try to look like someone who belongs here.

Spoiler: I do not.

At precisely 9:01, a door opens and a woman steps out. If she's over thirty, I'll eat my pocket square. She moves with the confidence of someone who owns the building. Her cheekbones could cut glass, her hair is pulled into a no-nonsense bun, and her eyes are gold-flecked, unblinking. This is Claudia Cowles, the woman who once made a Disney executive cry at a wrap party. Respect is too small a word.

"Mr. Hartley," she says, voice as cool and sharp as her features. She gestures for me to follow. "Come in."

Her office is all floor-to-ceiling windows and minimalism, a space that looks out over Los Angeles like it's daring you to prove you deserve to be there. She points to a chair. I sit, suddenly aware of every way a slouch, a twitch, or a nervous smile could ruin me.

She studies me. "Your agent says you're eager. Is that true, or just a PR spin?"

I swallow. "It's true. Ever since I landed in LA, I've been working three jobs to pay rent and taking acting classes at night. I'm here to level up, to break past the background roles and get out of day jobs that barely cover groceries."

Her lips curve into a smile. "Everyone says that. Why should it be you?"

I tell the truth. "I'm too stubborn to quit, and I have no fallback plan. If I don't make this work, I have to move back home and pick up a dead-end job to help my family."

She doesn't blink. "You ever betray a friend for a job?"

I pause, stunned. "I mean... no? I don't think so."

"You will," she says, and taps her pen twice against a notepad. "Would you lie to get ahead?"

I try to match her intensity. "Only if the truth would sink me."

"You're quick," she says. "That's good. There's no room for slow in this business. What do you know about Erin Cowles?"

I blink. "Your... sister?" I try to phrase it as a question, but the answer is obvious.

"Half-sister," she corrects, instantly. "She's brilliant. She's mysterious. She'll be your mentor if you pass."

I nod slowly, processing. "Okay. My resume's on the table. You know what I can do on screen."

"And off. I've seen the reels. I want to know what you'll do off-screen around her. Are you afraid of anything?"

I almost say no, but then: "Honestly? I'm terrified of being a disappointment."

The room is silent for a beat, then she stands, gliding over to the window. "You're interesting, Mr. Hartley. I like interesting. It's inconvenient, but it's memorable."

She faces me, her eyes sharp. "You'll come back tomorrow at seven. There's a cocktail hour for the new class. Wear something that won't embarrass me and don't be late."

I nod, and she waves me out.

The moment I'm back in the lobby, I call Tally. My finger hovers over her contact photo—her gap-toothed smile from before the diagnosis, when her hair still fell in copper waves past her shoulders.

She answers on the first ring. "Well? Did Hollywood fall at your feet yet?"

"I think I passed the first round," I say, relief washing over me. "But it was like being interviewed by a Bond villain."

She laughs, and it's the best sound in the world. A reminder of why I'm really here, why I left Portland with nothing but promises and desperation. "Did you tell them about the time you drank a whole bottle of ranch for a dare at Dad's funeral?"

"Tally," I groan, "I'm trying to be professional. And I thought we agreed never to mention that again." I duck behind a potted plant as a group of executives strides past.

"You know Mom's telling everyone at church you're starring in the next Marvel movie, right?" There's rustling on her end—probably her shifting around in her hospital blankets.

"Tell her to aim lower. Like, way lower. Background-extra-who-gets-eaten-by-aliens lower." I pause, lowering my voice. "How was treatment today, kiddo?"

"Boring. Nurse Jenna let me have two popsicles, though." Her voice gets smaller. "The medicine made me throw up after. Again."

My chest tightens. "I'm sorry, Tal. If this mentorship works out, the insurance—"

"It's okay," she interrupts. "Dr. Reyes says I'm being super brave. Says I'm his star patient." She yawns, and I picture her tiny frame drowning in the hospital bed, stuffed unicorn clutched under one arm. The one that Dad won her at the state fair five summers ago. "When you're famous, can you buy me a real unicorn?"

"First thing I'll do," I promise. "You feeling strong enough for me to read you Harry Potter tonight?"

"Only if I'm your date to the Oscars," she says, ignoring my question. "Oh, and call Mom sometime, okay? She misses you."

I promise I will, knowing I'll forget anyway. Just like I'm trying to forget how small Tally's hand looked when I last held it, wrapped in IV tape. Or how the medical bills are stacking up faster than my acting prospects, and this mentorship might be my last chance to be more than just another failed actor with a family who needs him to succeed.

That night, I lie in bed, staring at the water stain on my ceiling. I imagine what it'll be like, meeting Erin Cowles. The legend. The reclusive daughter of director Victor Cowles and actress Vera Moria. If I don't blow it, maybe I'll finally get my break. Maybe I'll prove I'm not a disappointment.

Maybe I'll survive.

CHAPTER THREE

ERIN

S unlight blinds me as I blink.

Is that ringing?

My head pulses as I groan into the pillow.

Banshee's Breath and fairy wine? Rookie mistake.

But it's not just the booze, though. It's the feeling of being a pawn in Claudia's latest scheme.

That noise...? Shit—it's the door.

I lie there for a moment.

Maybe they'll leave?

But the doorbell doesn't stop. I groan again.

"Alright, alright, I'm coming!" I shout, instantly regretting it. My voice bounces around my skull like a pinball at an arcade. I stumble to the door, hair a bird's nest, makeup smeared like war paint. My limbs feel like they're held together with string and Elmer's glue.

Whoever this is, they're about to get the wrath of a hungover fae.

I yank open the door—and freeze.

Liam. Fucking. Hartley.

All six feet of him, with that stupid sandy faux hawk, piercings, and warm brown eyes.

My mentee.

Fan-fucking-tastic.

He's standing there all bright-eyed, unreasonably chipper, and entirely too mortal to be knocking on my door at the ass crack of dawn.

"Uh... hi," he says, raising a cardboard tray like it's a peace offering as I rack my brain to recall the contract Claudia emailed me last night. "I wasn't sure what you liked, so I got one black, one with oat milk, one with... I think lavender? And a chai latte, because I panicked."

I stare at him. Not at the coffee—though I'm halfway to forgiving him for the sheer number of options—but at the fact that Claudia sent him here.

Today. This early. Without so much as a warning.

"You realize it's barely 9 a.m., right?"

He blinks. "I—yes? I thought we were starting today? Claudia said you were expecting me."

I give a humorless laugh, rubbing my temples. "Claudia also says kale counts as flavor and that I should wear beige more often. She's not exactly a reliable source."

Liam's grin falters. "So... this is a bad time?"

"No, it's the worst time," I say, stepping aside anyway. "But you're here. With coffee. So come in before I change my mind."

He steps past me into the apartment, doing that awkward, half-walk-half-hover thing people do when they're not sure if they should take their shoes off or sit down. My place is a chaotic blend of old books, designer furniture, and a kitchen that hasn't been used since the Obama administration.

"Wow," he says, glancing around. "This is... cool. Like, gothic-meets-magazine-cover cool."

"I was going for 'deeply exhausted woman who regrets paying rent,'" I mutter. I snatch a coffee at random and take a cautious sip.

Lavender. Ugh. Risk didn't pay off.

I grab the black coffee instead. He's looking at my bookshelf now, tilting his head at the rows of unlabeled glass jars and one obsidian skull. His hand starts to reach for it—

"Don't touch that," I snap. He startles.

"Sorry. It just looked... interesting?"

"It hums when it's working," I say. "House rule—don't touch things that hum."

He pauses. "That metaphorical or—"

I wave it off. "Do you want ground rules or a hospital visit?" He wisely backs away from the shelf.

"So," he says, sitting gingerly on the edge of my leather couch, "do we, uh... start with like a tour? Or... trust falls?"

I squint at him. "Do I look like the kind of person who does trust falls?"

He holds his hands up. "Fair. Icebreaker games?"

"You're cute," I say dryly. "But no. Let's establish a few ground rules instead."

He straightens, like a kid trying to impress the teacher. "Okay. Shoot."

"One: I'm not your friend. I'm not your therapist. I'm not your PR agent. I am your mentor because my sister wants to ruin my life and probably yours."

"Cool. Harsh but honest."

"Two: You'll keep your mouth shut about anything you see, hear, or overhear while you're around me. One breach and you're on your own."

He nods, swallowing.

"Three: No heroics. If things go sideways, you back out. No grand gestures. No dramatic sacrifices. Just keep your head down and your job intact. Got it?"

"Got it."

"And four..." I pause, fixing him with a stare. "Don't fall in love with me. It's tacky."

He sputters into his coffee. "Wha—I—I wasn't—"

"Relax, Hollywood. I'm kidding."

Mostly.

I wave a hand. "Kind of."

He sets his cup down very carefully. "Right. So, um. When do we start the whole mentorship thing?"

"Right now," I say. "Rule five: never show up at someone's place before noon unless you're carrying caffeine, currency, or bribes."

He grins. "What if I bring all three?"

Oh, he's cocky. This'll be fun. Or a disaster. Possibly both.

"Rule six," I say, grabbing my phone. "You're not ready for the real work. So until further notice, you're my assistant. Intern. Shadow. Whatever lets you follow me around without drawing too much attention."

Liam arches a brow. "You're letting me in by... making me your intern?"

"Exactly." I toss him a pair of sunglasses from a cluttered side table. "Put those on. We've got a gallery to hit downtown. Think: press event, but with wine, moody lighting, and people pretending to understand sculpture."

His expression is a glorious mess of confusion and awe. "Okay. Cool. Cool, cool, cool."

"You say 'cool' one more time, I'm leaving you on the curb."

He flashes me that actor-perfect grin. "Noted."

I chug the rest of my coffee, slip on a pair of stilettos that could double as daggers, and grab my keys. "Let's go, mentee. Try to keep up."

He follows me out the door with a bounce in his step.

Poor bastard has no idea what he's in for.

***

The gallery doesn't have a sign. Just a set of unmarked black doors in a brutalist concrete building that looks like it might house a villain's lair—or a really exclusive Pilates studio. Liam stares up at it like it might bite.

"This place has vibes," he mutters, adjusting the sunglasses I told him to wear. "Like... underground cult meets elite hedge fund."

"You're not far off," I reply, and push the door open before he can say something worse.

Inside, it's too quiet. The kind of quiet that feels like it's waiting. The air smells faintly of incense and something older—metallic, like rust.

Or blood.

The walls are bare concrete, broken only by massive, abstract sculptures. One looks like a bird mid-scream. Another is just a polished column of what might be bone. Liam stops walking.

"Is that real?" he whispers, pointing at the bone sculpture.

"Depends on your definition of 'real.'" I don't stop walking. "If anyone asks, it's resin."

He lingers behind, scanning the space like he's trying to decode something no one else sees. I glance back. He's stiff, alert. Still trying to play it cool. But I can see the questions starting to flicker behind his eyes. He's not just confused. He's noticing.

That's... dangerous.

I need him to relax. Or at least pretend to. A woman appears—just materializes from the shadows. Her white-blonde hair gleams under the dim lights, her dress layered in silk and spiderwebs. She smiles like she knows things I don't want her saying out loud.

"Miss Cowles," she purrs.

I force a nod. "Helene."

Her gaze shifts to Liam.

She tilts her head, curious and sharp. "And this would be...?"

"My intern," I say quickly. "He doesn't bite."

"Pity," she murmurs, eyes raking over him. "The eyes are nice. Shame about the rest."

Liam does a confused half-wave and smiles. "Uh. Thanks?"

I elbow him lightly. He flinches and smiles at her again.

Helene glides away, vanishing as seamlessly as she came.

I exhale.

Too fast. Too obvious.

I turn to Liam.

"Rule seven," I murmur. "If someone makes you uncomfortable, smile and nod. Don't flirt back. Don't take drinks from strangers. And if you see a mirror that reflects something wrong, don't look into it twice."

He squints. "Is that metaphorical or—"

"Sure," I say. "Let's go with that."

The second gallery room is darker. Spotlights fall like moons over the displays. A painting hangs on the far wall—huge, brutal, black and gold with slashes of red. A woman stands in the center, eyeless, crowned with thorns, her arms outstretched in something between a blessing and a curse. Liam steps closer.

"She looks like you," he says.

I freeze.

Just for a second.

"I get that a lot," I say. "It's not a compliment."

I can feel the painting's gaze even without eyes. The kind of art that remembers who looked too long.

Fuck curses.

He opens his mouth to ask more, but I catch a flash of movement from the corner of my eye.

"Stay here," I say quickly. "Look around. But don't touch anything that hums."

"Hums?"

I'm already walking away.

A man meets me near the sculpture hall—tailored suit, creepy smile.

A producer. Claudia's client. Of course.

"Erin, darling," he says, voice dipped in sleaze. "Claudia said you'd be bringing your little protégé."

"I'm not that little," Liam calls, a little too loudly from behind me.

Fuck my life.

The man's grin widens. "No. You're not."

I touch Liam's arm. "Go find the sculpture in the hallway," I say, too sweetly. "The one that hums when no one's watching. You'll know it when you hear it."

He gives me a weird look and raises a brow, but wanders off.

Good. I need five minutes.

The man leans in, his cologne cloying. "You're playing with fire, Erin."

"I always am," I say, sipping the champagne a server hands me. It tastes like citrus and subtle notes of blood. I glance over at Liam. He's crouched in front of the sculpture now, head tilted. Listening. Then he goes still.

Not confused—focused.

He heard it.

He's listening.

Something coils tight in my chest.

Not fear.

Not quite.

He fits here better than he should.

He's learning.

And that's a problem.

***

By the time we get back to the house, Liam's loosened up a little. Not a lot. Just enough that he looks less like he's waiting to get attacked.

"You okay?" I ask, unlocking the door.

He exhales slowly. "Just... not sure what to expect."

"That makes two of us," I mutter, pushing open the door.

The lights are low and warm, and the scent of something spicy and probably inedible is floating in from the kitchen. Music filters through the space—lo-fi, vinyl crackling, maybe on purpose.

There's a thud from deeper in the house, followed by a voice shouting, "IF YOU SET ONE MORE THING ON FIRE—"

A second voice: "It was an accident! The sage slipped!"

I sigh. "Well. They're here."

Liam gives me a cautious look. "You said this wasn't a party."

"It's not. This is just... them."

We step inside.

Wren appears first—barefoot, wearing a pair of ripped tights under cutoff shorts and a shirt that says YOUR AURA IS WEIRD. She's perched on the kitchen counter, swinging her legs like a child. Her eyes lock on Liam immediately.

"You brought a man home?" she says, dramatically. "Oh my god, is this a date? Are we being normal now?"

"Hi, Wren," I say.

"Hi, boss lady," she grins, sliding off the counter. "Who's this? Wait, let me guess—actor, obviously. That jawline has tax brackets. You're either a Taurus or emotionally repressed. Possibly both."

"Uh," Liam says. "Taurus."

"I knew it," she beams. "I can smell it on you."

There's a flicker behind her grin. Just for a moment. Something moving under the glitter, and I realize then she's thrown up her glamor. She reads people too well. Because once, not so long ago, she had to.

Before Liam can answer, André wanders into the room holding a protein shake in a mason jar, wearing basketball shorts, no shirt, and the smug confidence of someone who just benched his own weight.

Note to self: Warn them next time.

"Yo," he says, eyebrows lifting. "New dude. Sick."

He holds out a fist for Liam to bump.

"I'm Liam," Liam says, bumping it with visible hesitation.

"André," he replies. "Erin's, like… gym husband. You play ball?"

"Uh. I—no?" André nods like that's tragic. "That's fine. You've got good posture, though. Respect."

I raise an eyebrow. "Where's your shirt?"

"Laundry," he says, like it's obvious. "Also, Wren burned a hole in it. Sage fire."

"Your shirt attacked me," Wren mutters.

"Sure it did," I say, heading to the living room.

Wren plops down on the couch, pulling her knees to her chest. "So, Liam. You interning for Erin? That's intense. What's it like? Has she yelled at you yet?"

"She doesn't really yell," Liam says carefully.

"Hmm. She must like you then."

André crashes into an armchair with the full weight of someone who has never sat down quietly in his life. I cringe as I eye the drag marks on my carpet and thank the gods it wasn't hardwood.

He drops his protein shake on the coffee table and eyes Liam. "So you're trying to be an actor, right? Like, actual gigs and stuff?"

"Yeah," Liam says. "I'm just shadowing for now. Learning the ropes."

André nods. "Respect. Starting from the bottom. Gotta grind."

Wren grins. "Careful, though. Erin eats interns alive."

"Not true," I say flatly.

"Figuratively," Wren says, waving her hand. "Mostly."

Liam looks around the room, trying to hide his confusion beneath an exhausted smile. But I can hear his heart racing. He should be terrified.

So why does he look... curious?

Like he's excited to be here and wants to learn more.

Good.

Curiosity is manageable. Curiosity means he's not running.

Yet.

***

Wren's already halfway through Liam's birth chart by the time I start herding everyone toward the door.

"He's got strong fixed sign energy," she's saying as we exit the house. "Probably stubborn, secretly emotional, but pretends he's chill."

"I am chill," Liam mutters.

"That's exactly what someone who isn't chill would say," she sings back.

André jogs ahead to the driveway like we've just told him there's free pizza waiting, which—to be fair—we did.

"We taking your car or mine?" he asks, swinging keys around his finger. "I did legs today, so I'm not walking."

"I'm not risking my life in your car," I say. "We'll take mine. At least it has airbags."

"My car has airbags!" he protests.

"That function."

The city shifts around us as we drive, Hollywood's noise fading with each turn until we reach the alley that hides the place we're actually headed. *Just Another Slice* sits quietly at the end, nestled between a yoga studio and what might've been a pawn shop in a past life. Its entrance is modest, marked only by a crescent moon curled around a neon pizza slice.

Liam squints at the sign. "Is this... a retro pizza parlor?"

"Sort of," I say. "Less retro. More retro vibes."

Inside, the smell of fresh dough, garlic, and melted cheese wraps around us like a warm hug. Arcade machines hum and beep in the background, their pixelated light bouncing off neon signs and polished countertops. A flat screen plays *The Princess Bride* on mute with subtitles above the booths.

The owner always has that movie on loop.

Wren heads straight for her favorite seat—a booth under a photo collage of local school events, where a younger version of me grins beside her and André, hands sticky with sauce. Liam pauses in front of the photos.

"That's you," he says, pointing at one. "Wow."

"I was a wild child," I mutter, sliding into the booth.

A waitress I've known since middle school gives us a wave and drops a laminated menu in front of Liam.

"First-timer?" she asks.

Uh, yeah," Liam says, looking around like he's stepped into a time capsule.

"Get the double garlic knots," Wren says, flipping her menu without looking at it. "And the root beer float if you wanna see God."

"I'll stick with water," Liam says, tentatively.

André leans across the table, eyes serious. "Wrong move, bro. The root beer float slaps. It's like a cheat code for your soul."

"Noted," Liam says, nodding slowly.

I let them ramble, watching from behind my glass of soda as the tension bleeds out of Liam's posture, one joke at a time. He laughs when Wren tells a story about the time André tried to pick up a girl by doing push-ups in a club.

"It worked," André insists.

"She thought you were having a medical emergency," I remind him.

"She gave me her number!"

"Out of concern!"

Their arguing fills the booth with warmth. It's easy, the way it always is with us—chaotic, messy, layered with history. And somehow, Liam doesn't just keep up—he fits in. By the time the pizza arrives—bubbling hot and slightly too greasy—Liam's shed most of his awkwardness.

He's talking with Wren about bad auditions and nearly choking on laughter when André tries to explain his theory that pineapple on pizza is a personality test.

"It's not even about the flavor," André says, mouth full. "It's about dominance. You pick pineapple, you're an alpha. That's just science."

"You read that in *Men's Health*, didn't you?" Wren asks.

"I skimmed it."

Liam wipes his hands on a napkin and glances at me. "So... this is where you hide from the industry?"

I shrug. "Pretty much. It's home. Weird and loud and sometimes smells like burnt cheese, but home."

He nods, absorbing that. "I like it. It's real."

I freeze for a beat.

Real.

That word shouldn't hit as hard as it does. Most mortals see us like we're gods wrapped in glitter.

Not people. Not messy. Not real.

But I suppose that's part of what makes them want to join us. That and not knowing we're a whole different race. I take a sip of soda to cover the silence.

"Careful," I say lightly. "You keep that up, and you might just become one of us."

Wren winks. "Too late. Already wrote his name in my dream journal."

The second round of root beer floats hits the table like a sugar bomb from the gods.

Wren clinks her glass dramatically with mine. "To chaos, carbs, and emotionally unavailable icons."

"I'm right here," I mutter.

"You always are," she says sweetly, "but mentally? You're about as checked-out as they come."

Liam looks between us, eyebrows raised. "Was that an insult or a compliment?"

"Yes," Wren says.

André, who's halfway through his fourth slice and a conspiracy theory about why gym bros are misunderstood, wipes his mouth and looks at Liam. "So what's your angle?"

"My what?"

"You know. Ambition. Game plan. The five-year dream. Don't say 'I just want to act' or I'll throw this crust at your head."

Liam hesitates, and I can hear his pulse quiet down. It takes me a second to realize he's actually thinking, not just reacting.

"I want to be good," he says, quiet but honest. "At acting, I mean. Not famous. Not rich. Just... good. Like I earned it."

Wren whistles. "That's terrifyingly sincere. Are you sure you belong in this town?"

"I'm starting to wonder."

André studies him for a second, nods slowly, then reaches out and slaps him on the shoulder hard enough to almost knock his float from his hands. "Alright. You'll survive."

"Thanks?" Liam winces.

"That's his way of saying he likes you," I explain. "Aggressive affirmations."

"I'm emotionally fluent," André adds proudly. "In my own dialect."

Wren rolls her eyes but leans her head on André's shoulder anyway.

"He's our himbo," she says. "Harmless unless provoked."

"Also very huggable," I add, smirking.

Liam smiles, but I catch him watching us—watching me—like he's trying to piece together the dynamics of our group, the unspoken lines between us. He's not wrong to be curious. Because this—the three of us—we've been through hell together. Auditions, trauma, scandals, exile.

Things we'll never say in front of a mortal intern with a nervous laugh and big eyes. Still... I let him sit here. That means something. I almost say it. Almost let it slip that no one outside this booth has seen me like this in a long time.

That maybe I want someone new to see it. But I bite it back. Because wanting things? That's how they get you.

***

Later, after the pizza's down to cold crusts and Wren's stolen a poster from the bathroom ("It was just sitting there!"). We step out into the cool night.

"I'll drive your car back," André says, already catching my keys midair before I can argue.

"Excuse me?"

"So I can grab mine and bounce," he explains, like it's the most obvious thing in the world. "You live uphill. My legs are toast. Leg day."

"You chose leg day," I mutter.

"Greatness requires sacrifice."

Wren salutes us with two fingers and hops into a waiting rideshare like she's boarding a spaceship, blasting synth-pop as it pulls away. André rolls down the window as he buckles in.

"Don't do anything dumb, kids," he says, grinning at Liam. "And by dumb, I mean legally binding."

He peels off like he's in Fast & Furious. Liam and I are left standing in the street, bathed in neon reflections and the last traces of garlic-scented air. We're each carrying a takeout cup and a pizza box stacked with leftovers. Mine's nearly empty. His still has weight.

He glances at me. "Is he always like that?"

"Worse, actually."

We fall into step as we walk back toward my place, the streetlights painting gold halos on the pavement.

"So," he says after a while. "They're... intense."

"Understatement of the century."

"I mean it in a good way." He kicks a pebble along the sidewalk. "You've got a real thing going with them. Like... found family vibes."

I shrug. "They're chaos gremlins with boundary issues. But yeah. They're mine."

He's quiet for a beat. "You didn't have to bring me tonight."

I glance sideways. "No. I didn't."

"But you did."

"Don't make it a thing."

"I won't," he says. "I'm just... glad."

We walk a few more blocks in silence. A light breeze tugs at the hem of my coat. Somewhere in the distance, a siren wails, faint and fading.

"You fit," I say suddenly.

Liam looks over. "What?"

"With them. With us. You fit better than you should."

He laughs under his breath. "That sounds like a compliment."

"Probably is."

He doesn't push me for more. Just walks a little closer, like he's trying to match my stride without even realizing it. I don't tell him that tonight scared me a little. Because letting someone in? Letting someone human in?

It's never just dinner and banter and a photo on a wall. It's a door opening. And doors have a habit of swinging both ways. We're almost back when Liam speaks again, softer this time.

"So... you and André," he says, like it's a casual question, but not really.

I give him a sideways glance. "What about us?"

"Are you guys... a thing? I mean, everyone in the industry seems to think so. I saw a headline once—'LA's It-Couple Shatter Style Records at Cannes.'"

I snort. "That's because André wore an open suit with no shirt, and I wore a dress with knives sewn into the hem."

"Sounds iconic."

"It was. And no, we're not a thing. Never have been. The press just ships us because we look good standing next to each other and refuse to explain ourselves."

Liam nods, his expression somewhere between amused and deeply relieved. "Okay. Cool. I mean, not that it's my business. I was just curious."

"You were definitely fishing."

He holds up his hands. "A little. Guilty."

I should tell him more about the history, the rumors, the few times André's feelings almost crossed a line before we shoved them back where they belonged.

But instead, I just say, "We're family. The annoying kind. That's all."

He nods again, like that answer matters more to him than it should. "Thanks for telling me."

Then his phone buzzes.

Liam checks the screen, winces. "Sorry. One sec."

He answers, and even before he speaks, I can hear a voice—sharp, nasal, unmistakable—blasting through the receiver. "Liam! Where the hell are you?"

Liam pulls the phone slightly away from his ear. "Uh, walking home from dinner?"

"Well, walk faster or teleport, I don't care. You got invited to Lysander's Undead listening party, and if you don't get your ass over there in the next thirty minutes, I swear to God—"

Liam's face goes pale. "Wait, Lysander? *Lysander* Lysander?"

"Do you know another Lysander who owns a record label and throws parties that even the devil RSVPs to? No? Then MOVE."

There's a long pause.

"I—I—yeah, okay," Liam says, dazed. "Just text me the address."

He hangs up slowly, turning toward me with a sheepish expression. "I, uh. That was Jake, my manager."

"I gathered."

He rubs the back of his neck. "Apparently, I got invited to Lysander's album release thing. I have no idea how. I didn't even think he knew I existed."

I force a tight smile. "Big night, then."

"Yeah. I mean... I guess I should go. Right? I don't want to blow a chance like this."

"No," I say lightly. "Of course not. It's fine. You should go."

"You sure?"

"Absolutely. Go schmooze. Shake hands. Avoid the punch."

Liam hesitates, like he wants to say something else. Like he's reading the shift in my tone and trying to decide if he should push. He doesn't.

"Okay. I'll catch you later, then?"

"Sure."

He shifts his pizza box to one hand, raises his takeout cup in a silent toast, then seems to think better of it.

He offers them both to me. "Here. I don't want to bring food to a record label party."

I take them without thinking. He gives me one last look—hesitant, almost apologetic—then jogs down the street toward the main road, toward the glittering firestorm of fame he's trying to walk into. I stand there and watch him go until he disappears around the corner, swallowed up by headlights and city noise.

I don't move. I just stand there, alone under the street light, holding a cup and a box that aren't mine.

Liam's leftovers.

Like I'm just a convenient rest stop. Just a place he passes through on the way to something bigger.

I don't care.

I do.

I stare at the takeout cup in my hand as the ice melts.

CHAPTER FOUR

LIAM

I wake up sideways. My face is half-smashed into a throw pillow I definitely don't own, and I'm wearing clothes that look like they belong to a fancier, less disheveled version of me. My mouth tastes like gin and cigarettes. For a second, I simply lie there, blinking at the ornate ceiling, trying to remember how I got here.

Right party.

Lysander.

Lights.

Too much eye contact with a casting director who called me "adorably undercooked."

Classy.

I sit up slowly, spine popping in protest. Someone tossed a blanket over me at some point, which is almost sweet until I remember—this isn't Erin's house. It's Jake's place. He must've dragged me here when I couldn't find my Uber app last night. My phone buzzes on the nightstand.

Jake: *You didn't totally embarrass me. Proud of you. Try water.*

Jake (again): *Call me when you're alive. We need to talk casting.*

My heart skips at that last part.

Casting.

Still bleary, I stumble to the bathroom and splash cold water on my face. The mirror's too clean, too harsh. I look up, squinting through the hangover haze—and freeze.

There, right below my jawline, are two faint puncture marks. I lean in closer. My brain offers every rational explanation it can—mosquito bite, acne, shaving nick. But none of them hold. Especially not when the memory floods back.

A girl at the party.

Hair like silk.

Eyes too dark, too deep.

—She'd whispered my name and leaned in too close. I thought she was hitting on me—until her mouth brushed my neck and everything fuzzed. The room spun. Music and voices faded out. For a second, all I could feel was her lips and something...Then she was gone. And Lysander was there. Cool, composed, almost bored as he wrapped a silk scarf around my shoulders and said something like, "This one is spoken for." He'd waved the girl away with a flick of his fingers. Then Jake had appeared. Talking fast, herding me toward the door like he'd just remembered we had somewhere to be—

The memory flickers, disjointed and too strange to be real—but the marks are there.

Still red.

Still mine.

I touch them lightly.

Still me.

But something about that night doesn't sit right.

The lights. The way the room shifted when someone said Erin's name. Lysander's eyes never quite leaving me. The girl's voice—soft, lilting, hungry.

I rinse my face again, harder this time. Try to laugh it off.

Party weirdness?

Alcohol?

Maybe I'd been drugged?

Still...

Some part of me remembers. Even if I'm trying to forget.

***

By the time I get back to Erin's place, the sun's blazing and the street is painfully quiet. Her car's in the driveway. But the laughter and liveliness of yesterday? It's... gone. I knock once before trying the door.

It's unlocked.

Inside, the air is cool.

Still.

The hum of the fridge is the only sound. No Wren singing in the kitchen. No André yelling about carbs. No Erin muttering about coffee. Only silence.

"Erin?" I call out.

Nothing.

I wander further in, pausing in the hallway. Her bedroom door is shut. I don't knock. Instead, I find myself in front of the door to the basement. The one she never mentioned. The one I haven't opened.

I hesitate, hand hovering over the knob. Something about this feels personal.

Sacred.

Like stepping inside would mean crossing a line I'm not sure I've earned the right to cross. But curiosity... It's a disease. And curiosity has a way of making people reckless.

I glance back down the hallway—still no sound, no motion.

Just stillness.

I push the door open. The stairs creak under my weight as I descend into soft light. The basement isn't what I expected—no cobwebs or laundry piles. Just a studio.

Huge.

Open.

Lit by narrow windows that cast long, angled shadows across the floor. And a painting—it hits me like déjà vu.

A woman walking alone through a snow-drenched Manhattan street.

Shoulders tense.

Hair wild.

Surrounded by silence and neon. It's not labeled. It doesn't have to be.

It's Erin.

Every brush stroke screams her name. But more than that—my breath catches.

The style. The palette. It's the same as the painting in the gallery. The painting of the eyeless woman with outstretched hands.

Not a copy. But the same design. Same technique.

Erin painted that.

Suddenly, I'm not just intruding on her space—I'm unraveling something she never intended me to see. I step closer. My fingers twitch, like they want to touch the canvas just to make sure it's real. The colors burn: deep midnight, sharp gray, and blood-red bursts like open wounds.

It's beautiful. It's lonely.

I swallow hard. Yesterday she opened her world to me. Her friends. Her favorite pizza place. And then I left her standing in the street like none of it mattered. Like she didn't matter.

And now? Now I'm standing in the middle of her sanctuary, uninvited, looking at her in a way I don't think she meant for anyone to. I back away slowly, leaving the painting untouched. The light in the basement shifts. I think it's the sun. But part of me isn't so sure.

***

The room is cold. I stand alone on the taped "X" in the middle of the floor as three pairs of eyes study me from behind a folding table. The casting director. The producer. And Julian West. The man himself. He doesn't even look up at first.

Just flips a page and murmurs, "Liam, right?"

"Yeah." My voice sticks. I clear my throat.

"We're going to have you read Jack's big scene. The one with Olivia. You got it?"

"Yeah," I nod. "I've got it."

I don't.

Not on paper. But it's burned into me—seared into the marrow of my bones. I haven't stopped thinking about it since Jake said the words Midnight in Manhattan. I close my eyes.

Breathe in.

The bar.

The empty glass.

The quiet before she walks in.

Olivia.

Four hours from Manhattan, heels clicking like gunfire on tile. A ghost I asked not to haunt me. I open my eyes.

"You shouldn't be here." My voice is low. Careful. Almost trembling. Like the words themselves are fragile.

"I didn't ask you to come." I pause. Let the silence stretch. Heart racing. Sweat curls against my neck.

"You don't get it, Liv. You come from penthouses and catered brunches. From clean slates and clean breaks. Me? I got a niece who calls me Dad and a bar full of ghosts who tip in quarters." A breath. It catches halfway.

"I ghosted you because I meant to. Because this—whatever this is—doesn't survive in the daylight." I look down. Then back up.

Can't help it.

"You say you love me, and I want to believe it. God, I do. But if I let you say it again, I'll say it back. And I don't get to do that. Not when I know how this ends." I don't mean to let the last line crack, but it does.

The room stays silent. I stand there, hands clenched so tight my fingernails dig into my palm. I finally blink. My eyes sting. Julian leans back in his chair. His eyes meet mine—steady, unreadable. They linger longer than they should.

Then: "Thank you, Liam."

No smile.

No nod.

Just the words.

I nod once. "Thanks."

And walk out, struggling to catch my breath as I replay the scene in my head.

Outside, the sun is blinding. The traffic, the heat, the real world coming back into focus. I should feel amazing. But instead, all I feel is this weird hollowness.

My phone buzzes.

Tally: *Any drama? You famous yet?*

I smile despite myself and hit call. She picks up on the second ring.

"Well, well, if it isn't Hollywood Hartley."

"Hey," I say, my voice already softening. "L.A.'s... It's a lot."

She snorts. "Good a lot or therapy a lot?"

"Somewhere in the middle."

She giggles, and just for a second, the ache in my chest eases. I don't tell her about Julian West. Not yet, and I don't tell her about the script or the scene or how my hands still won't stop shaking. I tell her about the pizza place instead. About André and Wren and the way Erin looked at me when I said I had to leave.

Because that's what's stuck with me. Not the audition. Not the silence in the room. But the look on Erin's face when I walked away. I stay on the phone with Tally while the Uber pulls out onto Sunset.

"Did they make you talk to anyone named Chad who says 'manifest' too much?"

"No Chad," I say, grinning. "But I did meet a music mogul who wears velvet suits and calls everyone 'darling.' So... kind of the same."

Tally snorts. "You always meet weirdos."

"Says the girl who tried to name our Betta fish 'Bloodfang.'"

"I was six. And it suited him."

"He was orange."

"He had *rage*." Her laughter dissolves into a cough. Dry, but rough. I hold my breath until it passes.

"Are you on your machine?" I ask softly.

"Yeah," she says. Her breath comes a little shallower now. "I just hate the sound. It's a noisy robot."

I swallow hard. "Well, tell the noisy robot to be quieter. You're royalty."

"You tell him!" she shouts, giggling, but I can hear the strain in her voice.

She's trying to make me feel better, when it should be the other way around. We're quiet for a moment. The kind of quiet that stretches over distance and time.

Then: "I miss you, Liam."

God.

"I miss you too, Tal."

The last time I saw her, she was curled on the couch with a blanket and a bowl of ice cream she didn't finish. Her hair's still mostly there, soft and copper-brown like Mom's, but she's getting thinner.

Too much for eight.

And Mom... she's holding the house together with coffee, appointment schedules, and whispered prayers. After Dad died—construction accident, instantly—Mom changed.

She got quieter. I was fifteen and furious. Tally was too small to understand what she'd lost. I started working every job I could find. Stockroom, loading dock, and an extra in local ads. Saving up for the dream I couldn't name yet. Then one day, I left.

Tally was five when the diagnosis came.

Stage 3.

I'd just landed my first big role in a clothing commercial. I offered to come back. Mom told me not to. *"Make it mean something,"* she'd said. And maybe that's the thing I can't stop circling...

Am I chasing this for her? Or for me?

Tally clears her throat. "You still acting?"

"Yeah," I say, then shake my head.

Focus Liam.

"Auditioned for a big movie today."

"Did you cry?"

"A little."

"Then you nailed it." She yawns. "If you get the part, can I come to the premiere?"

"You kidding?" I say. "You'll be my date. Dress, crown, red carpet."

"Can it be sparkly?"

"Only if it blinds people."

She giggles. "Deal."

I glance out the window—Erin's street coming into view, her house tucked quietly beneath the trees.

"I gotta go," I say. "I'll call you tomorrow?"

"On a Wednesday? You promise?"

"Promise."

"I love you," she says.

"I love you more."

Click.

The car eases to a stop at the curb. I don't move right away. Just sit there, phone still in my hand, forehead pressed to the glass. I left to chase something bigger. Something that could rewrite our story. Give her the life she deserves.

Something that could make all the distance worth it. But the closer I get to it... The more I wonder if I'm running toward something, or just running away.

***

The front door creaks open as I step inside, the cool air washing over me. The house is quiet.

Maybe no one's home?

I kick off my shoes by the entryway and head toward the living room. That's when my phone rings.

Jake.

I answer it mid-step. "Hey, what's up?"

"Liam!" Jake practically shouts. "You fucking did it!"

I blink. "Wait—what?"

"You landed it, kid. Midnight in Manhattan. Julian West called personally. You're playing Jack."

I stop walking. It takes a second to process. "You serious?"

Jake laughs. "I haven't been this serious since I begged you not to dye your hair purple for that Hot Topic commercial. They loved you. That scene? You killed them."

I exhale—disbelief, joy, fear—all tangled in a single breath.

Jake continues; "This is your big break. Don't screw it up. Be smart, be respectful, and for the love of God, don't fall for your co-star."

"Right," I mutter. "Wouldn't dream of it."

He hangs up before I can say more. I lower my phone slowly.

Jack.

I'm Jack.

I glance toward the backyard. Through the glass doors, I see her.

Erin.

She's barefoot on the stone patio, paintbrush in one hand, wine glass in the other. A canvas sits propped on an easel in front of her, half-painted and glowing in the rosy evening rays. Her long black hair's pulled into a loose twist, cobalt blue streaking her cheekbone.

She looks... effortless.

She hasn't noticed me yet. I hesitate, fingers tapping once against the glass.

I have news. Big news.

And I'm suddenly not sure how she'll take it. I push the door open. "Hey."

She startles just slightly, then her expression relaxes. "You're back."

"I am."

"I thought maybe you got buried under rejection letters or swept off by a studio exec."

I grin. "Close. Jake called."

She raises an eyebrow, but doesn't say anything.

"I got the part," I say finally. "Midnight in Manhattan. I'm playing Jack."

For a second, she just stares at me, unreadable.

Then she blinks and sets her brush down. "Well, damn. Guess that calls for champagne."

Five minutes later, we're sitting on the patio under the string lights. She pops a bottle from a mini fridge I didn't know she had out here. The champagne is cold and sweet.

"To you," she says, raising her glass. "The boy who made Julian West feel things."

"To me," I echo.

She clinks my glass and takes a sip. I follow suit.

For a moment, it's easy. We chatter about our day and share stories about the entertainment industry. The kind of banter that makes you think maybe, just maybe, everything's about to get better.

"So get this," I say, setting my glass down. "Jack's this down-on-his-luck bartender raising his niece in upstate New York. He has this one wild night with a high-powered lawyer named Olivia—"

I stop. Because she's staring off in the distance, and her face is cherry red.

"Erin?"

She doesn't meet my eyes. Just swirls her champagne and takes another sip.

Then she says, too evenly, "I already know."

I raise an eyebrow. "What do you mean?"

Another long pause.

"I've already signed on," she says. "I'm playing Olivia." The world spins.

"What?"

"I didn't know," she says quickly, finally meeting my eyes. "Claudia pulled strings. Said it would be good PR—high-profile drama, strong female lead, all that. I signed the deal last week."

I sit back. Processing.

"So we're—"

"Costars," she finishes. "On-screen lovers."

The champagne bubbles between us. Fizzing in the silence.

"Is this bad?" I ask finally.

She laughs, but there's no humor in it.

"It's complicated. I'm supposed to be your mentor, remember? This whole arrangement was supposed to be professional. Structured. Safe."

"And now we're being paid to fall in love."

"Yeah." She takes another slow sip. The string lights glint in her violet eyes, but her mouth is drawn tight.

"They're going to love this," she says. "The PR people. The tabloids. The studio execs. 'Rising star mentored by legacy heiress turned co-star heartthrob.' It's practically pre-written."

I watch her. "So what do we do?"

She lifts her gaze. Her voice is calm, but there's tension beneath the surface.

"We act. We rehearse. We don't blur lines."

"Right," I say, swallowing the knot in my throat. "No blurred lines."

But I'm already thinking about the way her eyes glow under the lights. And the fact that we're about to cross every line we're pretending still exists.

CHAPTER FIVE

ERIN

T he air outside the soundstage smells like heat, dust, and too many egos crammed into one production lot. I step out of the black SUV and onto the concrete, already regretting the heels Wren convinced me to wear this morning. The haze clings to the ground—a stubborn fog of smog and sunlight—and the sun hasn't even had the decency to finish rising—but already, the place is humming with the quiet tension of a film set.

Then Liam arrives. He steps out of his car, backlit by the rising sun like something off a magazine cover. His expression is unreadable, but his eyes flick to me for just a second. And something inside me shifts. Annoyance prickles first.

Why does he look so calm about all this?

But beneath it, like a slow, sinking weight, comes another feeling. A flicker of attraction I keep trying to smother.

The awareness of him—his posture, the way he holds himself like he's bracing for impact.

God help me.

We exchange a nod.

Civil.

Professional.

Detached.

The mentorship. The co-starring roles. The PR campaign Claudia dumped in my lap like a lit match.

It's too early to process any of it.

"Coffee, boss?" a familiar voice pipes up. I turn, grateful, to see Todd Wells—my overly competent personal assistant—practically bouncing toward me with a tray of coffee in one hand and a clipboard in the other. Sandy-haired, bright-eyed, and with his headset already snug over his ears, Todd looks way too awake for six-forty in the morning.

"You're a lifesaver," I mutter, grabbing the cup from him.

"Latte, extra shot, oat milk, exactly one hundred twenty-four degrees," he says, not missing a beat. "I confirmed your wardrobe time with Wren. Your trailer's prepped and blessedly cold. The director wants to touch base after the read-through. And you've got three interviews I stalled for now—I told them you're getting method."

I raise an eyebrow. "Getting method?"

He shrugs.

"It works. They think you're intense. One of them even called you 'enigmatic.' Also—" He lowers his voice, leaning in. "Heads up—Claudia's been emailing the producers."

I stop mid-sip. "About what?"

"Unclear. But she wants regular progress updates on the film. Apparently, she's taking a 'personal interest' now."

My stomach sinks. "Of course she is."

"Don't worry," Todd says quickly. "I'm running interference, but I thought you should know."

Liam approaches just then, still scanning the set. His eyes land on Todd, then on me.

Todd offers a cheerful wave. "Todd Wells—personal assistant to the chaos that is Miss Cowles. Nice to meet you."

"Liam Hartley," he replies. "Intern and co-star to the chaos."

Todd chuckles. "He's funny. I like him."

"Don't encourage him," I say, brushing past both of them.

I can feel Liam's eyes on my back as I head toward the set. "Let's just get through today."

***

The set for *Midnight in Manhattan* is a sprawling maze of faux brown-stone backdrops, lighting rigs, tangled wires, and extras already in hair and makeup. Todd trails beside me, flipping through his clipboard and muttering reminders.

He flips a page. "Also, a letter arrived this morning from your father. It was delivered to your team directly—signed and sealed."

I nearly trip over a cable trying to get outside, bumping into Liam, who's following behind. "What?"

"Don't shoot the messenger." He holds up the envelope like it might bite him. "I haven't opened it. Thought you'd want to handle it on your own terms."

"Leave it on the table in my trailer," I say, voice tight.

Todd nods and thankfully changes the subject. "Julian West is on set this morning. Wants to meet you in person before the read-through. Just a handshake and a hello."

I spot him near the monitors, deep in conversation with a lighting tech. Julian West—cinema darling, camera-wielding genius, and the man who's supposed to direct my emotional spiral onscreen.

He notices me and, with a friendly nod, crosses over. "Miss Cowles. Mr. Hartley. Welcome aboard."

"Julian." I take his hand briefly.

His grip is firm, his smile calm. "Looking forward to it."

"Likewise." We part with a nod.

Then Wren's voice rings out: "There she is!"

I spot her waving us down from across the backlot near the wardrobe trailer, clipboard in hand and a mischievous glint in her eye. She's already in full chaos-mode, barking orders at assistants and rearranging racks with theatrical flair before racing across the backlot to us.

"Let's get you pretty," she squeals.

I groan. "Here we go."

"Come on, lovebirds," Wren chirps, grabbing both our arms. "Time to make you look fab-yuh-luhs."

I look behind me just in time to see Todd trying not to laugh. He waves goodbye and shouts, "Good luck," before disappearing.

Save me, someone.

Wren drags us back through the chaotic backlot. Everywhere I look, there's action. A harried PA sprints past, balancing a tray of coffee cups. Two grips argue over the placement of a massive light, their voices lost in the cacophony of power tools and shouted instructions. We weave through a maze of trailers and equipment cases. I catch snippets of conversation— gossip about an actress's latest meltdown, complaints about craft services, debates over camera angles.

It's a familiar chaos, the heartbeat of a film set. All the while, Wren chatters nonstop, peppering Liam with questions about his family, his hobbies, and his dreams. I half-listen, more focused on not tripping over the tangles of cables snaking across our path. We reach the wardrobe trailer, and Wren ushers Liam and me inside. It's a cramped space, every inch packed with racks of clothes, boxes of accessories, and the occasional glimpse of Wren's personal style—a sparkly top hat here, a pair of steampunk goggles there.

"Right!" Wren claps her hands, her grin turning downright diabolical as she glances at her clipboard. "So, I may have accidentally double-booked your fittings. Silly me! You'll just have to change at the same time. I'm sure neither of you mind, right?"

I narrow my eyes at her.

That conniving little—

"Wren," I hiss, "can I talk to you for a second?"

But she's already shoving us behind a flimsy partition, tossing outfits over the top. "No time! We're on a schedule, people! Chop chop!"

I turn to Liam, my cheeks burning. He looks just as mortified, his ears turning pink.

"I, uh... I can wait outside," he stammers.

"No!" Wren's voice rings out. "I need you both ready for makeup in ten minutes—director's orders!"

I take a deep breath, steeling myself.

"It's fine," I mutter. "Let's just... get this over with."

We turn our backs to each other, the rustle of fabric filling the awkward silence. I peel off my T-shirt, hyper-aware of Liam's presence behind me. My fingers feel clumsy, betraying the nervousness I'm desperately trying to hide. I hear Liam shifting behind me, the soft whisper of fabric against skin. My traitorous mind conjures an image of his broad shoulders and the lean muscles of his back.

Focus!

Professionalism, Erin.

You're a pro, dammit.

My elbow bumps against something solid and warm.

Liam.

I jerk away like I've been burned, mumbling an apology.

"S'okay," he murmurs, his voice low and husky.

The contact lingers longer in my memory than it should. For a beat, I don't move. His arm brushed mine for barely a second, but I can still feel the heat where it touched. My body's too aware of his.

Too reactive.

It's just adrenaline, I tell myself.

Stage nerves. And yet...

I shake my head, annoyed at myself.

It doesn't matter.

He's just another co-star.

Another pretty face.

I slip the dress over my head, trying to focus on the task.

Then Wren calls out, "You decent back there?"

"Yeah," I call back, turning around and finding myself face-to-face with Liam.

He's wearing dark jeans and a Henley that hugs his chest in a way that should be illegal.

Our eyes meet.

Time stalls.

The trailer door bangs open.

"Sorry I'm late!" a voice booms. "I brought pastries to make up for it!"

André strides in, all easy charm and ridiculous good looks. He's carrying a bag of pastries and a coffee, looking like he walked off a photoshoot.

"André!" Wren squeaks. "You're... here. Now. In this very small space."

André grins widely as he spots me. "Erin! There's my bestie!"

He sets the stuff down and hugs me so hard I leave the ground.

I laugh. "Put me down, you oaf."

He does, with a pout. "Is that any way to treat the guy who brought you butter-flavored heaven?"

André turns to Liam, offering a fist bump. "Hey, Liam! Long time no see. I'm playing the lovable ex-boyfriend. You must be the lucky bastard who gets the girl."

Liam bumps back, smiling tightly. "Nice to see you again."

Wren squints at her clipboard and mutters, "Oh, fuck me sideways with a cactus!"

We all stare.

"I triple-booked the fitting," she shouts.

Then, louder: "I fucking triple-booked the fitting!"

Chaos erupts.

"New plan! André, strip. Liam, finish and get to makeup. Erin, grab your shoes. Go!"

Clothes fly everywhere before she races out, slamming the door behind her. André shrugs, then peels off his shirt with a flourish. Even I can't help but stare for a second. After all, he's a Greek god with a tan.

"Damn, André," Liam whistles. "Do you bench-press trucks?"

"Kale smoothies," André replies. As André yanks off his jeans, Liam gets nudged onto my shawl.

"My bad," André says when he notices me tugging at it.

Without thinking, he yanks the shawl—and sends Liam flying. He crashes into me, pinning me against the trailer door. His arms are around me.

Legs tangled.

Heat.

Breath.

Eyes.

"Erin," he breathes, "are you okay?"

My brain doesn't answer right away. All I register is the solid weight of him. The closeness. The scent of citrus and cologne. I'm not supposed to feel anything, but I do. A soft panic. A flutter of something stupid and dangerous that settles somewhere in my throat. Before I can answer, the door flies open.

"Well, well, well," Wren says, smirking down at us. "What do we have here?"

I blink up at her. "Wren, I swear to God—"

"Comfortable?" she waggles her brows.

"It was an accident," Liam says, still cradling my head.

"Sure," Wren says. "Want me to come back in five? Or ten?"

André panics behind us. "Oh my God, I am so sorry!"

I finally manage to croak, "Help us up?"

Wren offers a hand. Liam stands first, then helps me up. I feel cold the moment we part. "We're fine," I mutter. "No harm done," I say louder. "Let's just get to the read-through before I die of embarrassment." Wren claps. "Places, people! We've got a movie to make!" I grab my script, willing my face to cool. The day's barely started. And I'm already in trouble.

By the time we make it to the read-through, my nerves are frayed. The chaos of the fitting room still clings to me like static. Liam's strangely quiet. André's grinning. Todd's already waiting, bless him.

"Read-throughs starting in five," he says, holding out a stack of scripts. "And you might want to fix your hair, Erin. You look like you've just wrestled a lighting rig."

I shoot him a glare. "I was tackled by a six-foot actor, thanks."

Liam clears his throat behind me. "Technically, André tripped me."

Todd grins. "Duly noted. Now go make sparks on the page."

We head to the read-through area—a makeshift circle of chairs and folding tables on the edge of the soundstage. The director, Julian West, is already there and wound up despite his laid-back sweatshirt and sneakers.

"Welcome to day one, everyone," he calls out. "Scripts out. Let's get into this."

Cast and crew settle into place. Liam ends up beside me, our chairs too close, our knees bumping. I pretend not to notice. André lounges on my other side, flipping through his script like it's a beach novel. Wren hovers at the edge, watching with hawk-like interest. Julian walks us through the first few scenes. I lock in, letting Olivia's voice slip over mine—cool, composed, utterly in control.

Until we reach scene seven.

Jack and Olivia.

The bar.

The first spark.

The dialogue dances between us:

"Did you steal this seat?" I ask.

"Wasn't using it for sitting," Liam replies, that crooked smile curling at the edge of his words. My breath hitches. Not from the line—but from the way he says it. From the way his voice shifts—just slightly—teasing and coy.

Like he means it.

Like Jack means it.

And I can't stop myself from meeting his eyes. He's staring at me. Our next lines fall out on autopilot. My voice is steady. His falters just enough to be real.

When the scene ends, silence hangs in the air. Then applause breaks out—scattered but enthusiastic. Julian raises an eyebrow.

"That," he says, "was electric."

Electric.

I should feel proud, but all I feel is exposed. Like someone peeled something raw and trembling out of me and set it under stage lights. And Julian saw it. Liam exhales beside me. I don't dare look at him.

André nudges my shoulder. "Someone's got chemistry."

I elbow him back. "Shut up."

But I feel it, humming beneath my skin.

That danger.

That pull.

Across the circle, Wren catches my eye. She's smirking. And I know—she saw it too. She always does.

"All right," Julian says, voice clipped. "Let's start scene eight. You're both already in character. Let's see what kind of mess they make."

Liam clears his throat. I brace myself.

"Olivia," he begins, voice soft. "This place always smells like gin and regret."

I glance up, startled by how easily the line slips out of him. It's not just acting—it's lived-in.

Real.

I flip to my cue. "That's because it's soaked into the walls. You can mop the floors, but you can't erase ghosts."

A murmur ripples around the table. I keep my face still, but my hand grips the script a little tighter. Liam looks up and meets my eyes. There's a flicker there—something gentle, something raw—and I look away too fast. We keep going.

Scene after scene, line after line. Jack and Olivia's story unfolds in quick, jagged strokes: flirtation, hesitation, connection, distance. It's us, rewritten in a Manhattan sports bar. There's a scene halfway through where Olivia confronts Jack after he disappears on her. It's supposed to be emotionally charged—tears, raised voices, tension like razor wire. I raise my voice, let it crack in all the right places. Liam leans forward, his knuckles white against the script.

"You think I ran because I don't care?" he says, almost too softly. "I ran because I do."

It punches the air right out of the room.

Silence.

Todd looks up from his phone; even Wren stops fiddling with the costuming notes on her tablet.

I hear André whisper a stunned, "Whoa."

I swallow hard and break the silence. "Can we—can we take a break?"

Julian nods. "Good instincts. Five minutes."

Chairs scrape.

Pages rustle.

I bolt.

I step outside into the sun-drenched corridor, gripping the edge of a windowsill until my knuckles ache. My heart is racing in a way that has nothing to do with caffeine.

That wasn't acting.

Not really.

At least... not for me.

Liam steps out a moment later. He's holding his script like it might catch fire.

"You okay?" he asks.

I nod, lying.

"That last scene..." he starts.

"It was good," I interrupt. "You were good."

He shifts on his feet. "You sounded like you meant it."

I force a laugh. "That's the job, Hartley."

He doesn't press.

Thank God.

I don't think I could hold it together if he did.

Wren pokes her head out. "Hey! Get your asses back inside!"

"Coming," I say, turning away before Liam can read my face again.

I'm not ready for what that scene meant. Worse, I'm not sure it was just a scene.

The rehearsal space is darker than the read-through room—intentionally so. The overhead lights are dimmed to simulate the bar where our characters meet again, the scuffed wooden floor slicked with faint stage tape marks. A few stools have been arranged like bar seating, and a worn-down sofa has been dragged in from props for the scene's climax. It's not a full set yet, but it's close enough to feel like we're already inside the movie.

I cross the space slowly, aware of every step, every glance. Liam stands on the opposite end, script still in hand but lowered, like he's already slipped into Jack's skin. André watches from the edge of the soundstage, arms crossed, chewing a protein bar. Wren flits in and out of view behind the lighting crew, taking notes on wardrobe adjustments and definitely not watching our every move. Todd is seated nearby, murmuring to someone from the script supervisor team, but his eyes keep flicking up to check on me.

Julian claps his hands. "Scene twenty-eight. Blocking rehearsal. Olivia confronts Jack at his bar, a week after he ghosts her."

He looks between us. "We're running this with full emotion. No props yet. I want to see where your bodies move before I let you touch anything. You hit your marks, you sell the pain, we make it work."

Liam exhales slowly and glances at me. "Ready?"

No.

Not even a little.

But I nod anyway. He steps into his starting mark behind the fake bar. I pace toward mine, slow and deliberate, heels clicking against the floor. Julian calls action.

I cross the imaginary threshold of the bar like I've just driven four hours in pouring rain. I channel Olivia's fury, but it feels so close to mine I'm not sure where the difference lies.

"Really, Jack?" I snap. "You disappear for a week, no text, no call, and I'm just supposed to what—forget you exist?"

Liam lifts his head, eyes already shadowed with guilt. "I didn't ask you to come here."

"But I did," I shoot back, my voice trembling in just the right places. "I drove four hours and walked into a bar I had to Google just to tell you that I—"

I pause.

Shit.

Breathe.

"That I love you."

The words hit the floor between us like a bomb. Liam's mouth opens slightly. He steps around the bar, toward me, his expression haunted.

"You shouldn't say that," he says, voice low and raw. "You don't know what you're asking for."

My chest tightens. "I'm not asking for anything, Jack. I'm telling you how I feel. Because I thought—"

My voice breaks. "I thought we had something."

Liam's hands twitch at his sides like he wants to reach for me and doesn't trust himself. He steps closer. We're toe-to-toe now.

"You don't get it," he whispers. "You showed up in a suit and heels and turned everything upside down. I've got nothing to offer you. No fancy apartment, no five-year plan. I've got bills I can't pay and a niece who's counting on me to keep the lights on. I can't love you the way you deserve."

"I never asked you to!" I shout, heat prickling behind my eyes. "I just wanted you to try."

Julian yells, "Freeze!"

We both go still.

"You feel that?" he says to the room. "That's what we're chasing. Rewind to the last five lines and walk the scene again, with full movement. This time, don't stop yourself. If you feel the impulse to touch, do it. If your character would shout, shout. We can rein it in later. But I need to feel it."

I blink hard.

Liam gives me a single nod.

Action.

I deliver the same lines, but this time I advance on him, fury in heels. Liam's voice cracks when he responds. The grief is real. The weight is real.

"You don't get it," he says again. "You have a life... a career. And I'm just trying to survive."

I take a shaky step forward. "Then let me be a part of it. Let me help you survive."

This time, when he reaches for me, his fingers graze my arm. I don't flinch. He grabs my hand, desperate, and for a split second, the air between us vanishes. His thumb brushes the inside of my wrist. My breath catches. It's Olivia's heartbreak on the surface.

But underneath that?

It's mine.

"Cut!" Julian calls.

Wren's chewing her pen cap, smiling like she knows.

Todd mutters something into his headset to the tune of: "We're going to need an intimacy coordinator, stat."

I step back, slowly, my pulse in my throat. No one moves. Liam and I just... stand there. Still holding hands. André lets out a low whistle

"Nice work," Julian says, satisfied. "Run it again after lunch."

As we break, Liam glances at me, his eyes unreadable. I look away. After all, this is dangerous, and we've only just begun.

I duck out of the soundstage, slipping past the catering table, the clatter of crew chatter, and Wren trying to get André to stop doing push-ups on set like it's a gym.

I need air.

Or silence.

Or maybe a sedative.

The truth is—I don't know what I need. Not when my pulse is still trying to punch its way out of my chest.

Todd catches my arm briefly on the way out. "Thirty minutes. Don't vanish."

"I'm just going to breathe," I mutter, already halfway gone.

I find a quiet corner behind one of the set trailers, where the sun filters through a fringe of palm trees and the hum of generators fades to a dull, manageable buzz. I sink to the concrete curb, legs outstretched, and let my head fall back against the trailer wall. My chest still feels tight. That scene—it shouldn't have hit that hard.

It was a script.

A fucking script.

I've done more emotionally draining scenes half-asleep with glitter in my hair.

But that look on Liam's face...

No.

Don't go there.

I tug my phone from my jacket pocket and pull up the Notes app. I'm not supposed to journal on set—it's a bad habit—but I need to dump this before it eats me alive.

Note to self: mortals are dangerous. They ask questions without asking.

They smile like they mean it. They touch your wrist, and suddenly your brain is jelly.

Liam Hartley is not real. Jack is not real.

This script is a job. Just a job.

I stare at the words, unsatisfied. I know I'm lying to myself. Still, I hit save. From around the corner, I hear the crunch of gravel and the soft creak of footsteps slowing down. I don't need to look up to know who it is.

His footsteps are lighter than André's, quieter. He hovers like someone with too many things to say and no clue where to start.

Liam.

He stops just before he rounds the corner. I can practically feel the weight of his presence pressing against the trailer wall. He's debating it—whether to come sit next to me.

I wait.

And wait.

But he doesn't come around. After a long moment, his footsteps retreat—soft, almost apologetic. I close my eyes and exhale. I wish I could say I'm relieved. But I'm not.

By the time I return to set, my nerves are pressed into a tight smile and stitched back together with coffee and denial. The sun's shifted in the sky, throwing long shadows across the makeshift set. Crew members swarm the space like bees in dark T-shirts, re-taping marks, adjusting lights, and prepping cameras. Liam's already back, pacing near the prop bar, his script folded and crumpled in one hand. He looks up when I step onto the soundstage—just a flick of his eyes, not quite a greeting. I give him a nod. That's all I've got right now.

Wren appears at my side, clipboard in one hand, iced matcha in the other. "You look like you survived. Barely."

"Don't I always?"

"Mm," she hums, nudging her drink toward me. "Sip?"

I take a grateful swallow of whatever witchy green concoction she's brought, letting the cold shock my system back into focus.

"Liam was circling this set like a sad puppy the whole break," she adds lightly, not looking at me. "Thought he was gonna wear a groove in the stage."

I ignore the way my heart sinks. "He's method. Leave him alone."

Wren smirks. "You're worse at lying than you are at making small talk."

Before I can respond, Julian claps his hands and yells, "Positions!"

Like a well-oiled machine, the crew scurries into motion. I glance around for Todd and catch him scribbling something down next to the director. His brows furrow as he watches Julian bark technical instructions—the guy might be just my assistant, but he absorbs this industry like he was born into it.

"Scene twenty-eight again," Julian calls. "But this time we go past the fight into the fallout. No holding back. I want tears. I want truth. If your heart doesn't ache by the last line, I've failed as a director."

Great. No pressure.

I take my mark. Liam does the same, hands now shoved into his pockets. I can practically see him shifting gears, slipping into Jack's skin.

The lights above us dim. The boom mic lowers. A hush falls.

"Action!"

This time it's different. He speaks first—the same lines, same blocking—but slower. Like Jack's afraid his words might crack the world in half. And I respond... not as Erin, not even fully as Olivia, but as something in between. Someone who wants to believe in people again. Someone who is terrified to.

I feel the tremble in my voice when I say, "I'm not asking for perfect, Jack. I'm asking for you."

Liam's throat bobs as he swallows.

His fingers twitch at his sides. "What if I don't know how to give you that?"

"You learn."

Our gazes lock, and something changes.

It's like the air between us twists.

Pulls.

Magnifies.

There's no acting anymore.

His hand reaches for mine.

Not on script.

My breath catches.

Not on script.

And then Julian's voice cuts through: "Cut."

Julian approaches, his eyes wide. "That... was something. That was real. Keep that rawness. Bottle it. We shoot it for camera Monday."

He checks his watch. "On second thought, take five and practice."

Crew scatters. Liam heads to the side, script still in hand, while I drift toward the edge of the lot, where the scaffolding for Monday's set is half-built, still smelling like fresh paint and sawdust.

"Erin," Julian calls after me. "Run that kiss scene with Liam. Just the beats and lines. No pressure. Let it simmer."

Let it simmer. Great.

Liam approaches, uncertain. "We okay?"

I nod. "Let's just do it."

We stand beneath the structure where Monday we'll shoot our first onscreen kiss. Right now, it's just a frame—but already it feels too intimate. Too quiet.

We run the lines. At first, it's mechanical. Rehearsal, plain and simple.

But then... I feel it...

His voice softens. My breath slows. We reach the part in the script—the build-up to the kiss—and neither of us moves.

Then it starts raining.

Out of nowhere, like the sky split open. The crew yells, scrambling for covers and tarps, but Liam and I duck beneath the low awning of the mock fire escape, trapped together in a pocket of dry air just big enough for two.

He's close. Closer than we've ever been. I can hear the rain pounding.

We keep running lines, quieter now. More raw.

"I wasn't supposed to fall for you," I say, Olivia's voice tumbling out of my own mouth.

"And yet you did," Liam replies—no, *Jack* replies.

But there's no Jack anymore. There's just him.

His hand brushes mine, not scripted. My breath catches. Neither of us pulls away.

A moment passes—not long enough, too long—and I find myself staring at his lips. Script pages are still in my hands, damp at the edges. But I'm not reading anymore.

He's not either.

He takes a breath. "Monday we kiss."

I nod. "Monday."

But right now... we're standing so close, it might as well be today.

The rain drums against the scaffolding. Our scripts hang limp in our hands, forgotten. I can feel the warmth of his arm next to mine, the way his breath hitches just before he speaks again.

"Erin?" he says, voice barely above the storm.

But I don't answer. I can't. If I open my mouth, I might admit something I can't take back.

Then—

"Erin? Liam?" A voice calls across the lot.

I yank my hand away like I've been burned. Liam flinches, like I actually did hurt him.

Julian's voice carries through the downpour. "You two okay? We lost power to half the set!"

We step out from under the awning, blinking into the mist as crew members swarm toward a smoking lighting rig. Someone's yelling about a blown generator. Sparks dance along the edge of a tarp as they yank cables from the puddles. Chaos.

But I barely see any of it.

Because I'm still standing too close to Liam. And his eyes are still locked on mine. And for a second—just a second—I think he might kiss me anyway.

He doesn't.

Instead, he runs a hand through his soaked hair and mutters, "Guess that's our cue."

I nod again, numbly.

As we head back toward the soundstage, the space between us stretches, taut and full of everything we didn't say. Every missed heartbeat. Every almost.

Behind us, the rain starts to ease. But inside me, the storm's only just begun.

CHAPTER SIX

LIAM

"Maybe," I say, trying to play it cool, "our chemistry was a little too good out there. Starting to wonder if we might actually be dating."

Silence.

The kind that drags like a dropped mic in a church.

André flinches. "Dude..."

I turn—and freeze. Erin stands ten feet behind me. No expression. Just a stare. She blinks once. Slowly.

Then she bends down, picks up her script from the floor, and walks away. No words. No acknowledgment.

André lets out a low whistle. "You just detonated your own love life, my guy."

My mouth opens, then closes again.

"I was joking," I mutter.

He sips his smoothie and shrugs. "So was the Titanic—right before the iceberg."

I watch Erin disappear into the shadows of the soundstage, that sinking feeling blooming in my gut.

God, I'm such an idiot.

I should've just said, "Good scene", and walked away like a normal human being. But no—I had to ruin it.

I take off after her, dodging crew and light rigs, desperate to fix whatever the hell this is. But I don't get far. She's already slowing down near the edge of the lot, one hand fishing her phone out of her back pocket.

She answers on the second ring. "This is Erin."

A pause.

Then her entire posture shifts.

"What happened?" she asks. "When?"

I stop a few feet away.

She doesn't look at me. Just turns slightly.

"I'll be there soon." Her voice cracks on the last word as she hangs up and stares at the pavement.

I step forward. "Erin?"

She flinches.

"What is it?"

She hesitates, then exhales through her nose. "My mother's nurse called. She collapsed again."

Shit.

"Do you want me to—?"

"No."

She starts toward the parking lot, fast and silent. I follow anyway.

"Let me drive," I say. "You're shaking."

"I'm fine."

"You're not."

She stops at her car door, keys in hand, trembling hard enough that she fumbles them.

"Fine," she bites out. "But no talking."

I nod, unlocking her car and guiding her in.

No small talk. No apologies.

Just the engine starting and the silence stretching between us as I drive.

Her fingers tap against her phone screen as she frantically texts someone. The farther we drive, the more the city gives way to winding roads and manicured hedges, until the Cowles estate comes into view like something out of a dark fairy tale.

I glance at her. She's staring out the window, lips pressed tight, but the glass reflects more than just the trees.

When we reach the gates, she punches in the code with shaking hands.

The gates creak open.

And we're in.

Inside, the mansion is silent. Not peaceful—just... tense. Every sound echoes. Portraits line the hallway, all stern faces and stiff smiles. Erin's in some of them, standing in front of a man and always on the edge.

A nurse meets us halfway down the corridor. "She's awake. Asking for you."

Erin nods and pushes past without saying a word. I follow.

Her mother's bedroom is a strange mix of hospital and home. Beeping monitors are tucked between designer curtains and high-backed chairs. She lies in the bed, pale and still.

"Mom?" Erin says, stepping forward.

She stirs. Her eyes open, searching, then land on me.

She murmurs something to Erin. I can't hear what.

But I see Erin's shoulders tense, then sag. She brushes a hand over her mother's hair.

"Just rest," she whispers.

We step into the hallway again. It's quieter now. Heavier.

"She was vibrant," Erin says. "Back before she got sick. She'd sing to me in French when I couldn't sleep. She traveled. Painted. Threw parties just because the weather was nice."

I nod.

"She's been disappearing for years," she says. "Bit by bit."

She swallows, eyes still fixed on the floor.

Then she looks at me, and I can see the pain.

"I don't know how much longer I can take this," she says.

I place a hand on her shoulder. "She's okay. You'll be okay."

She closes her eyes for a second.

Then nods.

Just once.

***

Back at the house, the silence feels different.

More tired.

Erin drops her bag by the door and heads straight for the kitchen without a word. I hover awkwardly in the living room until she calls out, "Can you grab my sketchbook? It's on the coffee table."

"Yeah," I say, already stepping forward.

Except... it's not on the table.

I bend down and spot the edge of a box sticking out from underneath. Old. Worn. Not hidden well, but definitely not meant to be seen.

I hesitate.

I should leave it.

Instead, I lift the lid.

Newspaper clippings. Photos. Medical records. The kind of thing you bury, not file.

A headline blinks up at me: *Victor Cowles' Hidden Daughter*. Another: *Tragedy at Home: Two Sisters, One Terrible Accident*. And then there's a photo—Erin as a kid, standing beside a younger version of her mother.

Vera.

Then I hear her behind me.

"Liam?"

I scramble upright, nearly spilling the box in my panic.

"Shit—I didn't mean to—"

"To what?"

She's in the doorway now, eyes unreadable as the reality of what I've done hits her.

"To dig through things that don't belong to you?" Erin replies, narrowing her eyes and crossing her arms.

"I tripped," I say, lame even as I say it. "I wasn't trying to dig through anything. I was just looking for the sketchbook."

She walks over without a word and sets the lid back on the box.

"You want to know something, then ask. Don't dig," she snaps.

"I'm sorry."

She doesn't reply. She just takes the box with her and leaves the room. The door to her studio shuts behind her with a soft click.

I slump back on the couch, face hot, chest tight.

I fucked up.

Again.

And this time, I'm not sure sorry will cut it. I pace my room. My phone's in my hand, clenched tight, thumb hovering over Tally's number. Erin hasn't said a word since the studio door clicked shut.

No yelling.

No texts.

Just nothing.

I sit on the bed and press the call button. It rings once.

"Liam!" Tally's voice is way too bright. "You didn't forget it's Wednesday, did you?"

I try to laugh. It comes out strangled. "Wouldn't dream of it."

"Because last time, you blamed jet lag."

"I was busy."

"You were playing pool with your manager!"

I sigh. "Okay, fine. I'm an ass."

There's a pause.

"You sound weird. What's going on?"

I flop back, phone pressed to my cheek. "I messed up. With someone. Bad."

"You finally fart in public?"

"Worse."

I hear her shuffle in the background—sheets, maybe.

Then softly: "Tell me."

I stare at the ceiling. "There's this girl—Erin. She's impossible and brilliant and intimidating and... kind of amazing. But I said something stupid. Then I... found a box. Stuff from her past. Articles, photos. I shouldn't have looked, but I did."

Silence.

Then: "Wow," Tally says. "You're a bigger idiot than I thought."

"Thanks."

"I mean, I love you. But yeah—you're a dumb dumb sometimes."

I press my palms into my eyes. "I know, and I tried to explain, but I don't think she's gonna forgive me."

"Did you tell her why you did it?"

"Because I wanted to know her better?"

"No, silly," she says, giggling. "Because you like-like her."

"I didn't say that."

"You didn't have to. You only act like this when it's about a girl."

I pause.

"...Okay. Maybe I like-like her."

"Thought so," She says, then continues. "Now stop being dumb. You can't fix this with flowers or a dumb apology. If she's a nice person, then she's been bullied her whole life. Don't be another meanie."

I nod, throat tight. "I know. So what should I do?"

"Stop being dumb and tell her the truth. Tell her you like-like her and be nice to her."

I blink and realize I'm getting solid dating advice from my little sister. "You know... you're weirdly wise for an eight-year-old."

"I watch lots of Hallmark and TLC with Mom."

"God help me."

She laughs—small, breathy, but real. It tugs at something in my chest.

"I love you, dork," she says.

"I love you too, Bug."

"And Liam?"

"Yeah?"

"Don't mess this up. She sounds awesome."

I smile into the phone.

"She is."

The house is too quiet. After I hang up with Tally, I sit there for a while, cycling through apologies in my head. Every version sounds worse than the last. Finally, I give up and go to her. Her studio door is slightly ajar, a soft halo of light spilling out beneath it.

I knock.

Silence.

I knock again.

"Erin?"

Still nothing.

"Look, I know I'm the last person you want to see right now," I say through the door. "But... I need to say something. And I swear, if you tell me to go, I will."

A long pause.

Then her soft voice: "Door's open."

I walk in. The studio smells like paint, wine, and lavender. Erin's perched on a stool in front of a half-finished canvas, brush in hand but not painting—just staring at it. She doesn't look up. I clear my throat.

"I'm sorry I went through your things. Really sorry. I shouldn't have. I was just... and after everything that's happened, I've been confused. Then I found the box, and I..." I trail off.

She still doesn't move.

"I didn't mean to hurt you," I add. "I j-just... wanted to understand."

She exhales slowly and sets the brush down. Her fingers are smudged with green and ochre.

"You want to understand, Liam?" she says quietly. "Alright."

She stands, wipes her hands on a rag, and finally looks at me. Her violet eyes aren't cold anymore—just tired. Like someone who's held the weight of the world on her shoulders for far too long.

"My parents were childhood sweethearts—Victor Cowles and Vera Moria. My mom was an actress. She was beautiful, brilliant, and reckless. My dad was a big-deal director. But they both came from powerful families who had already picked out their future spouses. Political marriages. The kind that aren't about love but legacy." She glances at me, gauging my reaction. "They defied them for a while. I was born out of that romance—and all while my dad was still engaged to Claire. His family forced him to go through with it anyway."

My throat tightens, but I don't speak.

"After I was born, my mom fought to stay on the Cowles estate as his mistress. She'd already been disowned and stripped of everything. Despite this, Victor kept his engagement, and Claire married my father. Not long after, Claudia was born. Then Nathan. We were all raised under the same roof... except it was never a home." Her voice drops. "Claire hated me. Hated my mother. Hated that Victor never loved her like he loved Vera. She took it out on all of us, but especially Claudia and Nathan. She made them feel like they were never enough to earn their father's love. My mom... she stepped in. Raised all of us."

She takes a breath. "Then... the fire."

My stomach knots.

"We were five. Claudia and I were playing in the living room, trying to climb the fireplace mantel like idiots. I tried to... boost us up. Something went wrong. We both fell, but Claudia landed deeper in the hearth. She got burned. Bad." Erin presses her lips together, eyes distant now. "Claire walked in as I was dragging myself out. She saved Claudia. But she never forgave me. She blamed me for everything."

"Claudia went through surgeries and therapy. She still has the scars. And Claire—well, Claire's fury needed somewhere to go." She meets my eyes and smiles as tears start to well up. "Christmas Eve, that same year. No one else was home. Claire dragged me downstairs. Said if I liked fire so much, I could have it. Then she threw me into the fireplace."

I flinch.

"She used the poker to keep me there. Hit me. Burned me. Every time I tried to crawl out, she'd beat me back in. Eventually, my mom came home. She found us. Pulled me out. Attacked Claire. Everything went to hell." A tear slides down her cheek. She doesn't wipe it away. "Claudia watched. She didn't stop her mom. Didn't cry. Just... watched."

"My mom took me away after that," Erin says, glancing out the window. "We left the estate. I had surgeries. Physical therapy. I was out of the spotlight for years. Until she got sick. She tried to hide it, of course, but she became weaker. And when she couldn't take care of herself anymore... we had to go back."

I exhale slowly. "Jesus, Erin..."

"I'm not telling you for pity," she says sharply. "I'm telling you so you understand why I am the way I am. Why I keep people out. Why I don't let people in."

Her shoulders sink, anger giving way to exhaustion.

"I'm tired of pretending I don't care. But I can't afford to care too much. Not with people like Claudia looking for something to use against me."

"Can I help? I want to."

She laughs bitterly. "That's what scares me."

I reach for her hand, and she lets me take it.

"Just tell me what to do," I say.

She doesn't answer. But she doesn't let go. And for now, that's enough.

CHAPTER SEVEN

ERIN

I'm not brooding. Really—I'm not.

I'm just staring a hole straight through my script. The pages are worn now, the corners soft and curling from overuse. I've read the same line three times, but nothing sticks. My thoughts are elsewhere, unraveling fast. Because he's laughing again.

Liam.

He's across the set, casually leaning against a lighting rig like he's made for it. That stupid, crinkle-eyed smile of his aimed at some grip who's halfway to smitten. He doesn't have to try. He belongs here—without effort. The crew loves him already. I hate how easily he fits in. How natural he looks. How badly I want to be the one he smiles at like that.

It's not jealousy—not entirely.

It's longing. For comfort. For ease. For someone who sees me and doesn't run. I start pacing, the script clenched in my hand. My boots strike hard against the concrete.

I need to move. Need to push the ache somewhere it won't bloom.

"Erin!" His voice cuts through the hum of the set like a live wire. I freeze.

Hearing my name in his voice—it's too much. But I turn anyway. *Because I always do.*

He jogs over, all bright-eyed and boyish, script in hand. "Got a sec to go over lines?"

I nod.

Of course I do.

We duck behind a half-constructed wall. The scent of sawdust hangs in the air, grounding.

Familiar.

Noise blurs—just a faint chorus of tools, footsteps, chatter. He starts flipping pages, mumbling a line under his breath but glancing up at me every few seconds. We try to run lines.

Try.

I stumble. Get distracted by the way he says "Olivia," like it means something. Like affection wrapped in velvet. With each read-through, he steps closer. And I let him. My skin buzzes, knowing how close he is. Electricity waiting for a spark. He mutters something. I laugh too loud, too honestly, and for a moment it's easy.

Too easy.

Like comfort is meant for people like me. Then he leans in. And I feel it—that gravitational pull, the kind that says we're headed for a collision we can't survive. He starts to speak.

I tilt toward him, breath catching—

CLATTER.

A clipboard crashes. A production assistant scurries past, apologizing in stammers. Liam bends and hands it back with a grin. I stand still, heart thudding, trying to pull myself back from the edge of something I don't have a name for.

"Saved by the bell," he says.

I smile too fast. "Or cursed by it."

Bitterness creeps in before I can stop it. Because the truth? I was going to let him kiss me. And I don't know what I regret more—the interruption or the fact that I didn't make the first move.

***

The makeup trailer is quiet. Dim vanity lights reflect in the mirror, casting everything in soft shadow. It's just us again. He's watching me in the mirror. The brush trembles in my hand.

Then his hand is there, brushing a strand of hair behind my ear like it's nothing before he straightens my necklace. But it's everything. His finger grazes my collarbone.

Suddenly, the door slams open.

"Shit—sorry!" The makeup artist's arms are loaded with palettes and brushes as she rushes to set up.

I flinch like I've been shot.

"Need water!" I choke out, latching onto the excuse, and bolt.

Outside, the sun burns overhead, but I'm cold. The kind of cold that creeps under the skin and stays. I hover by the craft services tent, gripping a lukewarm coffee, chasing a stillness that won't come.

Then her voice cuts through. "Erin!"

Claudia.

Of course.

She's storming across the set.

"You're needed for family matters," she announces, already grabbing my arm.

The day spirals from there. Scenes derailed. Schedules warped. Her voice in my ear. By the time I snag a second behind the wardrobe tent with Liam, I'm shaking.

"I am this close to strangling her," I mutter.

"She's got claws, huh?"

"You have no idea."

But maybe he does. The way he watches me—me, not the act—is too careful to be casual. Then Todd appears, clipboard in hand, tablet under one arm.

My shadow.

"Wardrobe's ready, Erin. Wren wants you in ten. Liam, you too."
He squeezes my shoulder.

"You need anything?" he asks, low enough that only I hear. I shake
my head.

"Not unless you can rearrange families."

"Not yet." He says as I turn away.

***

I duck out and cut around to the back of the stage. The air back here
is cooler, and here I'm finally alone. I breathe in a lungful and exhale
the memory of his hand nearly on mine. But it's not nearly enough.
Wren's voice finds me before I spot her. She's on the fire escape,
pacing, her curls flying around her.

"No, you listen, Collin," she hisses. "I am not coming over. Because
I have work. Because I am at my job. Yes, the same job you think is
beneath you. Oh my god, can you even hear yourself?"

She hangs up mid-sentence, then throws her phone into her bag.
That's my cue.

I climb the metal steps as quickly as my boots can take me.

"You know, if you shatter the screen, that's, like, seven years' bad
luck," I offer, sliding in beside her.

Wren's face is a mosaic of exhaustion and rage, but she manages a
wry smile. "It's fine. It's still under warranty, unlike my relationship."
She leans into the railing, eyes fixed on something in the parking lot.

"Collin?" I ask, like I don't already know.

"Collin," Wren confirms, spitting the name like it's spoiled food.
"We're done, by the way. Officially. He said I was 'too intense' and
then had the nerve to suggest I quit my job so we could travel on his
trust fund."

I wince. "That's a new flavor of condescending. Did he offer to pay you an allowance?"

"Oh, absolutely. He said, and I quote, 'You could focus on your hobbies, babe.'" Wren makes finger guns and mimes shooting herself. "My hobby is not dying of boredom in some Italian mansion, so I passed."

We both watch as an intern speeds by below us, toting a box of vegan donuts. Sporting platform heels as she races through the gravel lot.

Only in Hollywood.

"You ever feel like you're just collecting red flags?" Wren finally asks.

"Constantly," I say.

She snorts, then glances at me sidelong. "What about you? Did you and the tall drink of skater boy finally make out in craft services, or are you two still crushing?"

I frown. "Wren, we are not a CW pilot."

"You sure about that? Because the way you were looking at him earlier, I was about to pull out some popcorn."

I try to play it off, but my ears are hot. "He's... nice."

"Oh my god, just say you want to climb him like a tree."

I flick a rock at her. "No, but thanks for the visual. That's definitely not going to haunt me."

She grins, but her eyes flick away, down to the lower lot where André is stretching in the afternoon sun. He's in full gym mode—sleeveless, golden, oblivious to the effect he has on anyone with a pulse. Wren's smile smooths out, goes quieter.

"You should tell him," I say.

Wren makes a face. "Tell who what?"

"André. That you're into him."

She laughs, but it's thin. "Yeah, sure, I'll just pencil myself into his harem. Get in line behind the other sixteen girls who want a slice of that fae cake."

I lean closer. "He likes you, Wren. He always has."

She shakes her head. "No, Erin. He likes you. Everyone knows it. You're the only one who doesn't see it."

I don't have a comeback for that. Not one that doesn't sound like a lie.

Wren sighs. "It doesn't matter. He's with Cecilia now, anyway. She's pretty and normal, and her mom doesn't send her on blind dates with trust-fund sociopaths."

"Isn't Cecilia a model?"

"Yeah, but, like, a nice model. I think she even eats food sometimes." Wren shrugs, half admiring, half mourning. "I'll survive."

André glances up then and sees both of us. He waves—just a little flick of the wrist—but it's enough to make Wren break into a toothy grin, if only for a second. She waves back, then mutters, "Ugh, I'm disgusting," under her breath.

"You're not," I say, bumping her shoulder. "But your taste in men is, maybe, a little tragic."

"That's rich coming from you, Miss Forbidden Fruit."

I stick out my tongue. "At least mine aren't misogynistic trust-fund babies."

We dissolve into laughter, loud and echoing off the fire escape, and for a moment, it's enough. It's enough to forget that both of us want something we can't have.

***

The day ends. The sun dips low. Golden light paints the edges of the set, but I can't feel it. I told Todd I'd walk myself back.

I lied. I just didn't want company. Didn't want Claudia to find me again. But she always does. The trailer door opens without knocking.

"You're moving into a hotel."

I blink slowly. "Excuse me?"

She steps inside and places a hand on her hip.

"I've already made the arrangements," she says. "Check-in is this evening. You'll be closer to set. No excuses for delays."

"I haven't been late."

"You've been distracted." Her eyes cut toward the set.

Toward Liam.

"And too close to the boy."

"He has a name."

"I don't care." Her words land like a slap.

"He's human. He's beneath us. And his presence is becoming... problematic."

"You mean it's becoming visible."

"Exactly. The press is already sniffing. And Father? He's losing patience."

I laugh, hard. "When hasn't he been on the verge of disowning me?"

"This time it's serious. Fix this, or you're out. No inheritance. No name. No protection. You'll be no better than a rogue." It might as well be a threat. Not just exile.

Erasure.

"So what?" I ask, voice low. "You just shove me into a hotel and expect me to vanish?"

"I expect you to remember your place." Her voice softens. Not kinder—worse.

Pitying.

"You were a scandal before you were even born. Vera was barely tolerated. You're barely tolerated. Stop making it harder than it has to be."

"I'll... I'll think about it." But we both know I won't.

She nods. "Do that."

Then, at the door: "And stay away from the human. You're embarrassing the entire family."

The door clicks shut. I collapse into the vanity chair, staring at a reflection I barely recognize. My burn scars shimmer faintly at the collarbone.

Covered, never hidden. She didn't even look at me. Just through me. I want to scream. Break something. Tear the script to shreds.

Instead, I just sit.

Still. Silent. Exhausted.

***

The hotel room is too quiet. So I leave the TV on for background noise. Something low and pointless, a sitcom with a laugh track. But it doesn't drown out the day.

And it definitely doesn't drown out her voice.

I dig out my journal, flipping past pages of half-written thoughts and scribbled reminders until I find a clean sheet. My handwriting's messier than usual, more jagged. The pen feels heavier in my hand.

I'm here now. In a hotel I didn't pick, living a life I'm not sure I chose. Claudia says it's for the best. For appearances. For the family.

But when she says "family," she doesn't mean me. She means the performance of us. The version that photographs well and stays out of tabloids.

I pause, tapping the pen against the paper, my mind drifting.

She said Father's on the verge of disowning me. Part of me wishes he would. At least then it would be over—the pretending, the tightrope walking, the guilt of being born from love that wasn't allowed to exist. Vera would've said we were a miracle. Claudia thinks I'm a curse.

I draw a little fire poker in the margins and immediately scratch it out. My chest tightens just looking at it.

I saw the way Liam looked at me today.

Not just on set—though that would've been enough to send my heart into a full-blown spiral—but later. When Claudia had her claws out. He was watching me. Not with pity. Not even with curiosity. With concern. And maybe something else. Something I can't afford to name.

I chew on the cap of my pen, then write the words I've been avoiding:

I want to trust him.

The moment it's on the page, I hate it. I hate the softness of it. The hope. I underline it anyway.

But he's human. And I can't. Not really. Not with everything I've seen. Not with what I am.

I've lived enough to know mortals never stay. And if they do, they want things I can't give. They demand pieces of you until you're hollowed out and smiling, just enough to keep them from seeing what's missing.

I close the journal before I can write anything more. Then I peel off my clothes and climb into the unfamiliar bed. The stiff white sheets are tucked too tight, like they're trying to restrain me. The city glows faintly through the window, humming with life I'm not part of tonight. I stare at the ceiling for a long time, thinking of Liam's stupid, lopsided smile.

The way he doesn't laugh when I flinch. Or how he looks like he wants to kiss me, but doesn't. And then I think of Claudia. Of the look in her eyes when she said I was embarrassing the family. Like I was a stain she couldn't scrub out. A story better rewritten.

I don't cry. I don't scream. I don't do anything. I just lie there, aching and alone, and promise myself:

Tomorrow I'll do better. I'll play my part. No one ever said the girl with the scars gets to keep the boy.

CHAPTER EIGHT

LIAM

Lights blind me—white-hot and unforgiving—as the set swarms with bodies. Crew members shout over the chaos, scrambling in every direction.

"Where's the scarf? She needs the scarf!" Claudia shrieks, hovering over Erin and barking orders at anyone within reach.

We're about to shoot a pivotal scene—one where my character finally confronts hers. The gravity of it is enormous, but the atmosphere is electric for all the wrong reasons. It feels like standing inside a viper's nest.

I edge toward the railing, repeating my lines under my breath, forcing myself to focus. The rebar wavers under my weight. My fingers tense around the metal; a jagged edge slices into my palm. Blood blooms—slow at first—then dark crimson against the waterfront backdrop. I barely feel the sting before Erin's whole body goes rigid. Her face drains of color, eyes going wide. She sways—and for a moment I think she's going to pass out, before she spins away and pukes over the opposite railing.

Gasps ring out. I take a step forward, but she bolts—fleeing the set like her life depends on it.

"Medic!" someone shouts behind me.

I stand there, hand dripping, still reeling. The crew swarms in around me. A nearby grip presses a cloth into my hand and wraps it tight.

"It's not that bad," I mutter.

But nobody's listening. The medic arrives—calm, efficient—and inspects the wound.

"You'll need stitches," he says. "You'll have a scar, but nothing major."

I nod, but my mind is already elsewhere. As they work on my hand, I keep glancing toward the exit, trying to make sense of Erin's reaction.

The concern must have shown on my face, because Julian pats my shoulder and says, "She'll be fine. Just needs a minute."

But five stitches later, Erin is still avoiding me.

The next two days are infuriating. Every time I enter a room, Erin finds a reason to leave. She reschedules our scenes, stays on the far side of the set, and refuses to look me in the eye. Her silence is louder than a scream, and by the third afternoon, I've had enough.

I wait until the crew breaks for lunch, then head straight for her trailer. My hand still throbs under the bandages—a dull, angry ache that reminds me of everything we're not saying.

I knock.

Once.

Twice.

Eventually, the door cracks open. Erin stands in the threshold, arms crossed tight over her chest. Her face is pale, lips pressed into a hard line. She looks like she hasn't slept in days.

"What happened back there?" I ask, my voice low.

She doesn't answer right away. Her eyes drop to the floor, and her fingers dig into the sleeves of her hoodie.

"I don't know what you mea—"

"Bullshit." The word comes out sharper than I mean it to.

Too fast.

But I don't take it back.

Not this time.

I step inside. She doesn't stop me. Instead, Erin turns away, shutting the door behind her with a soft, defeated click. Her shoulders sag—just a little.

"Blood," she says quietly as she crosses the room. "It brings back... memories."

She stops near the small kitchenette, standing stiffly with her back to me. Like if she doesn't look at me, maybe I'll go away. I don't move. I wait.

"My sister's accident. My own," she mutters. "I'll never be able to look at blood the same way again."

The words hang in the air between us, and guilt punches hard in my gut. I step forward instinctively, reaching toward her—but then the door bursts open behind us. Claudia stands in the doorway. Her eyes lock on me—cold, sharp, full of hate and disgust. I watch her fingers close around Erin's arm.

Erin doesn't flinch. She doesn't argue. She lets herself be pulled away like this isn't the first time. Like it's routine. I stand there, stunned and furious. Watching them disappear. Watching the door slam shut behind them. And I know—this isn't over. Not by a long shot.

***

Claudia's voice cuts across the soundstage before Julian even calls action. "Let's make sure there's no stage blood around. We wouldn't want Erin to faint and ruin another scene."

A few crew members laugh. Others look away. Erin freezes beside me, her eyes locked on the floor.

Claudia advances, clipboard in hand. "Wardrobe—aim for sexy, not whore."

Erin says nothing. She just stands there, fists tight at her sides. At the monitors, Julian finally intervenes.

"Claudia," he says, calm but firm, "mocking her in front of the crew isn't helping the production—or anyone."

Claudia turns with a smile sharp enough to draw blood. "Julian. I didn't realize you were still pretending to be in charge."

Julian crosses his arms. "I am in charge. And if we're going to stay on schedule, this harassment needs to stop."

She cackles. "Schedule? Please. This film is a disaster, and I'm trying to salvage it. If you had the spine to direct, maybe I wouldn't have to."

He stands firm. "Mocking her isn't getting this film anywhere."

Claudia's smile doesn't waver.

She leans in, her voice low and deliberate. "Keep testing me, Julian, and I'll call Father. Let's see how fast you're replaced."

He doesn't back down, so she adds, louder this time for the entire crew to hear: "Especially when Daddy's name is on the checks."

That one lands.

Several crew members glance away. No one says a word.

Satisfied, she turns to the crew. "And just so we're clear—for consistency, all notes to Erin go through me. She's too childish to take direct criticism."

I move to step forward, but Erin catches my wrist in a silent plea. *Don't.*

Claudia sees it.

"Touching," she says, amusement lacing every syllable. "A knight in shining armor."

Erin lets go, her face unreadable. But I can feel the tension. Claudia takes a step closer to Erin.

"You know," she adds, "some people just aren't built for the spotlight. Even if they were born into it."

Erin stares straight ahead.

Claudia tilts her head. "But don't worry, sweetie. A little stage fright never killed anyone's career."

Still, Erin doesn't break. She simply turns and walks off set—quiet, composed.

Claudia claps her hands once, loud enough to get the whole set's attention. "Alright, everyone—back to your places. Let's try not to embarrass ourselves this time."

***

By Thursday, the set is a wreck. The whole crew walks on eggshells around Claudia, afraid to be her next victim.

"You call that acting?" she sneers across the soundstage, folding her arms. "I've seen mannequins with more emotion."

Erin's lower lip trembles. Her eyes shimmer—but she doesn't break.

Not yet.

We reset the scene. She misses her mark by inches.

"You're pathetic!" Claudia shrieks.

Then she slaps her. The sound echoes across the set. Erin stumbles back, falling to the floor with a thud.

"Take five," Julian shouts.

The crew scatters like roaches. Erin rises slowly, a crimson handprint blooming across her cheek. She doesn't say a word as she turns and flees. I follow her, trying not to punch something.

At her trailer, I pause.

The door is cracked open. Inside, her voice is small. "Nathan, I really need your help with Claudia... she... she hit me... she's ruining everything."

A pause.

"I know she's untouchable. But if someone doesn't step in, she's going to ruin the whole film. Can you talk to her or Father? Please?"

Another pause.

I can hear her tapping her nails on something.

"I know," Erin says, voice tight. "But we can't just kick her out. She has too much pull."

Another pause.

"Okay," she says. "Hopefully things smooth over. Thanks, Nathan."

Click.

I open the door before she notices. Erin turns around, startled—wide-eyed like a cornered deer.

"This ends now," I say, fighting to keep my voice calm.

She turns to run, but I step in her way. "I don't care if she's your sister—no one deserves to be treated like that."

Her gaze darts around the room, avoiding mine.

"You don't understand," she whispers, backing up until her shoulders hit the wall.

"Then help me understand," I say, stepping closer. "Why do you let her do this to you?"

Her lips part, then close again. Her whole body shakes.

"Erin." My voice softens. "Talk to me."

She looks up at me, exhausted and glassy-eyed. Then she slowly sits on the couch, hiding her face in her hands.

"You're not going to let this go, are you?" she asks, voice muffled.

I shake my head. For a moment, the only sound in the trailer is her uneven breathing. Then I notice her shoulders shaking. She lowers her hands slowly, wiping her face with the heel of her palm.

Her eyes are red, lines streaking through her makeup as she stands and crosses to the mirror above the small vanity. She dabs under her eyes with a tissue, steadies her breathing, and adjusts the fall of her hair.

Then, meeting my reflection in the mirror, she speaks again. "Fine. You want to help?"

I nod.

"Let's go to *Just Another Slice* for lunch."

I blink. "The pizza place?"

"Yes," she snaps, then softens. "Away from here. I just need some air."

Before I can answer, she grabs her bag and slips past me.

"Okay," I say, falling into step behind her. "Let's go."

I half-expect Claudia to appear and drag her back, but the set is eerily quiet. We make it to my car without incident. She slides in without a word. I climb into the driver's seat, fumbling with the keys. The silence in the car is overwhelming. I keep glancing over at her—the fading mark on her cheek, the tension in her shoulders. I grip the steering wheel as I try to think.

"Do you want to talk about it?" I ask. She doesn't turn to face me—just stares out the window, eyes fixed on her reflection in the glass.

"I just need a break," she finally says. "A break from all of it."

I nod, even though the pain in my chest twists tighter. She doesn't want to talk. That much is obvious. But sitting next to her in silence makes me feel like I'm failing her anyway. I want to fix every-thing—say something that could ease the hurt she's carrying.

But I don't know what to say without making it worse. She doesn't need saving. She needs space. And I don't know how to give her that.

We pull up to *Just Another Slice*, the neon sign casting a orange glow over the sidewalk. Erin is out of the car before I can say anything. I scramble to catch up as she pushes through the glass door with a smile on her face.

I hesitate.

Just for a second. I watch the tension drain from her shoulders as she crosses the parlor, like she's walking into a place that actually feels safe.

But then she glances back.

"You coming?" she calls, already halfway to the counter. I stare at the pavement for a beat, the city humming around me like it's waiting for my answer.

This is what you fought for Liam, I remind myself.

Not just the chance to know her—but to be someone she might finally let in.

I roll my shoulders. Exhale slow.

Of all the ways I pictured this moment ending, "trauma pizza" wasn't on my bingo card, I think as I step through the door.

CHAPTER NINE

ERIN

The pizza parlor buzzes around us—arcade games chirping in the background, while the neon lights washing everything in a nostalgic glow. Liam and I sit across from each other, the promise of melted cheese and greasy comfort briefly making me forget the circus my life has become. A large pepperoni for him, a supreme for me. I can almost taste the liberation.

As I pick up my first slice—cheese stretching in perfect strings—Liam clears his throat. "So, about Claudia—"

My face falls. My eyes snap to his. "Seriously? Right when I'm about to eat?"

He raises his hands in mock surrender, but his eyes stay fixed on mine. "It's just... I've seen what she does. And the things happening on set—it's weird, Erin."

I sigh, the pizza cooling in my hand. "It's what she does best—manipulation and control."

"Why don't you just leave?" he asks, like it's the simplest thing in the world.

I set my slice down, knowing I have to give him something if I want him off my back. The parlor's cozy atmosphere makes me feel braver than usual. "She's forced me into a hotel near the set, Liam. If I don't cooperate, she'll have my father to cut me off."

He looks at me, genuinely confused. "Then why not just—"

"Walk away?" I finish for him, the words bitter and familiar. "I'm working on it. But breaking free from the Cowles family isn't as simple as packing a suitcase."

He leans closer, his slice forgotten. "What do you mean?"

"I've been making my own connections. Secretly selling my artwork to save money." I pick at my crust. "It's just not enough yet."

He watches me, his concern both frustrating and strangely relieving.

"I'm not as fragile as you think," I say—more to myself than to him.

He finally takes a bite, nodding slowly. "I know."

I watch him, wondering how much he's already pieced together. How much longer I can keep hiding the truth from him. So I feed him a watered-down version—just enough to keep him content. Half-lies wrapped in honesty. The more I talk, the lighter I feel.

"Honestly, the stuff you're seeing on set isn't helping," I admit, relieved to finally say it.

Liam leans back, the metal chair creaking beneath him, eyes locked on mine like he's assembling a puzzle. "But what is it, really?"

I hesitate, searching for the right spin. "This is going to sound insane," I say with a small, conspiratorial grin. "But you know how people in this town can be a little... intense? A lot of them thrive on theatrics."

He raises an eyebrow. "That's one way to put it."

"Like the gallery back then," I continue, "Helene and many others? They love dressing up, acting like characters. It gives them a huge power trip—their very... eccentric."

Liam studies me, a slow understanding spreading across his face. "So you're saying it's all just... Hollywood theatrics?"

"Pretty much," I say, relieved he's buying it. "I mean, you've probably seen cosplayers in other places. Here, some people here make it a lifestyle—they get their kicks from being different or edgy. It makes them feel powerful, I guess."

He tilts his head. "And you? You don't get sucked into it?"

"Do I look like I have the patience or desire to dress up in black lace and be mysterious? I'm sitting here eating pizza with you, not at some exclusive party with a bunch of wannabe celebrities," I say, finally taking a bite. The taste is as glorious as I'd hoped—home sweet home baked into the crust.

He laughs. "I guess this place is full of surprises."

I shrug.

"I'm surprised you didn't expect it. This is Hollywood, after all. Half of us get paid to dress up as monsters; other people make it their whole life." I finish, trying to appear nonchalant, secretly savoring the fact that this is the first real laugh I've heard from him in days. The conversation ebbs into carefree banter, the tension of untold secrets erased by the safety of pepperoni and arcade games. I watch him devour his slice, wondering how long it'll be before the truth becomes impossible to hide—and whether he'll still be sitting across from me when that time comes.

But Claudia's threat lingers, making me restless. "We should get back to set before Claudia declares me a missing person," I say, tossing some bills onto the table.

He gives me a long, searching look as we stand. "You know... I'm here if you need me," he says, his voice serious again.

I smile and open the door, letting the sounds of the street wash over us. "Thanks," I say, stepping outside and leaving the safety of the pizza parlor behind. "But this is something I have to handle on my own."

***

Back on set, things are somehow worse than ever. Julian huddles with the production assistants while the crew scrambles for flashlights and backup generators. Confused shouts and muttered curses fill the air. It feels like someone wired the building's electrical system into a haunted house attraction. Cameras malfunction mid-scene, screens warping into distorted images before snapping to black. Sound techs frantically adjust equipment as the microphones pick up eerie static instead of dialogue. The unsettling atmosphere greets us like an old ex.

I notice the disturbances intensify every time Claudia walks into a room. Lights flicker, and equipment sputters out with even more dramatic timing. Finally, after the third consecutive equipment failure, Julian calls for a ten-minute break while crew members whisper theories ranging from faulty wiring to Mercury retrograde.

I struggle to keep my composure, fingers fidgeting with the hem of my sleeve as I watch Claudia speak with the production assistants across the room. Her demeanor is as cool and unruffled as ever. She catches me staring and offers an eerie, knowing smile. Suddenly, every light on set cuts out at once, plunging us into complete darkness. In the chaos of shouts and fumbling crew members, a hand finds mine. A thumb brushes the back of my hand in slow, calming strokes.

Eventually, flashlights appear, and the crew manages to rewire a section of the set that's been neglected and tangled for ages.

The lights flicker back to life, blinking a few times before finally holding steady. Liam and I step apart quickly before anyone can notice. Julian's voice cuts through the chatter as he tries to rally the crew—strained but still hopeful. "Alright, people! Let's get this under control!"

I barely have time to gather my bearings before Claudia starts making her way toward us. Liam shoots me a worried glance, but

I just smile back. I'm not cracking. Not yet. Claudia's halfway to us when Julian calls her name.

"Claudia!" His voice is a mix of desperation and exasperation—the perfect bait.

She pauses, glaring at us as if daring me to get any closer to Liam.

"The two of you look awfully cozy," she says. "Enjoying the show?"

She doesn't wait for a response—just narrows her eyes.

"I suppose rats can survive anywhere," she sneers.

Liam opens his mouth, but I nudge him to stay quiet. Claudia turns on her heel, her irritation obvious as she stalks back to Julian.

I watch as she joins the huddle, but even she can't hide the fact that things on set are unraveling. I take a deep breath, the tension in my shoulders easing just a fraction.

With Claudia occupied, the set finally begins to settle. The lights stay on, and the crew begins reassembling with cautious optimism. Equipment comes back to life, cameras and monitors flickering on. The eerie static fades, replaced by crisp audio checks and relieved murmurs. We return to our places, the set buzzing with renewed purpose. Julian barks out orders, his confidence returning with every successful test shot. Claudia stands beside him, her frustration barely masked by her schooled expression.

As we resume filming, I try to focus on the scene—on anything but the looming threat of Claudia and the secrets I'm keeping from Liam. But as the cameras roll and dialogue fills the air, I can't help but wonder how long this fragile calm will last.

Not long enough, apparently.

A couple of hours later, I'm gripping the railing of a boat dressed up as a luxury yacht, the deck swaying underfoot. Wind tangles my hair, the black water swallowing the glow of the city behind us. The rolling motion flips my stomach and my knees wobble.

"You're green," Liam murmurs from just behind my shoulder. Before I can protest, his hand closes gently around my arm, steering me away from the bustle of crew members checking lights and rigging cameras. He settles me near the stern, away from the chaos, and drapes his jacket around my shoulders without a word. It smells like cedar and laundry soap.

I breathe.

Slowly.

The nausea eases, replaced by a bone-deep fatigue I hadn't realized was there until now.

We stand there in the hush, waves slapping the hull, stars trembling in the water's reflection. For a rare moment, no one's watching.

"You ever feel like you've got the whole world on your shoulders?" Liam says finally, eyes fixed on the horizon. " My sister. She's sick, and they're counting on me to pay for her chemo. If I screw this up—" His voice fades into the wind.

Something in my chest tugs. "Sometimes I feel like I'm just... playing a part they wrote for me," I say. "Like no matter what I do, I'm still his daughter. Still theirs to use."

I instantly regret saying it. But Liam doesn't push. His hand stays a few inches from mine on the railing—close enough to feel, not close enough to cross the line.

Julian's voice cuts across the deck, calling for places.

The moment breaks.

We walk back toward the glow of the set lights, my fingers brushing the scar at the curve of my ear—a reminder of what I can't tell him, no matter how much I want to.

***

Later that night, my hotel room has the ambiance of a freshman dorm mixed with a Vegas bender. Wren sits perched on the edge of my bed, her curls wild and her cheeks flushed from two generous pours of fairy wine. André sprawls on the couch, one leg slung over the armrest, his golden hair falling into his eyes as he watches a mindless cable rerun. I'm on the carpet, back braced against the mini fridge, knees drawn up. For once, the world outside feels like a distant rumor.

"Do you think the guy from *The Bachelor* is actually here for love or just the free tequila?" Wren asks, eyes glued to the TV.

"Statistically? It's tequila," I reply, and she snorts, sloshing her glass and nearly baptizing the nightstand.

André, who has been silent for an hour except to request more snacks, suddenly stiffens. His phone vibrates, a blue glow cutting across his face. He glances at the caller ID.

"Be right back," he mutters as he slips out onto the balcony.

It's only the three of us tonight. It's our tradition: a bottle of something questionable and a bad reality TV show every Saturday night. But as I watch André's broad silhouette through the balcony glass, a pang of worry stirs. I grab my hoodie and follow him out.

The city glimmers in the distance, a million tiny stars.

André leans on the rail, phone pressed to his cheek. "Yeah. No, it's fine. I get it."

Silence, then: "You don't have to explain. It's not a big deal."

He hangs up without waiting for a reply and looks out over the city.

"Trouble in paradise?" I ask.

He barks a tiny laugh. "She dumped me. Tried to do it over text."

"Wow. Classy."

He shrugs, not looking at me. "Cecilia's always been efficient."

I fold my arms and lean beside him on the rail. "You okay?"

André's eyes, normally bright and vibrant, are flat and dull. "I don't know. I guess so. Honestly, I was expecting it. She only really liked the money and the parties."

I snort, but he doesn't smile.

"You liked her," I say, more gently.

He shakes his head. "Liked the idea of her. Liked the way people looked at us when we walked in together, you know? Like we were the couple everyone else wanted to be." He spits over the side, then watches it fall. "But she never got me. Not the real me."

"You mean the guy who loves to work out and watch trashy TV?"

That earns me a half-smirk. "You know me too well, Cowles."

We stand in silence then, watching the hotel's blue pool lights flicker up and down the walls. The city's neon lights smear across the horizon. I hear Wren's giggle through the doorway, followed by the clink of her glass on the side table.

"She was just another girl," André says quietly. "I only knew her for a few months. It's not like... whatever."

But I'd seen the way he'd looked at Cecilia when he thought no one noticed. A hunger for something real, even if he pretended it was nothing.

"You're allowed to feel shitty," I tell him.

He doesn't reply. Instead, he grabs up the half-empty bottle of fairy wine from the table and downs the rest in three gulps. He wipes his mouth, then types something into his phone.

"I'm going out," he says, dialing.

His voice brightens with a strange, fake cheer. "Alexis? It's me. You still up?"

I lean on the balcony, watching his back as he disappears into the hallway. For a moment, I wonder if I should go after him, but the look on his face tells me he wants to be alone for a while.

Back inside, Wren is watching *Titanic* with a glassy-eyed expression.

She looks up and tries for a smile, but the effort collapses. "Where's André?"

"Gone to get trashed and meet someone named Alexis," I say.

She nods, her lower lip trembling. "Cecilia left him, didn't she?"

"Yeah," I say. "But he'll live."

Wren wipes her nose with the back of her hand. "Why do I have to be in love with a playboy who doesn't even notice me?" she asks, her voice small.

I slide in beside her on the bed and wrap an arm around her shoulders. "Because you like a challenge."

She tries to laugh, but it comes out as a sob. "I'm such an idiot."

"Nah," I say, pulling her close. "Just a romantic in a city full of cynics."

We sit together in the flickering TV light, the soundtrack swelling as Jack and Rose attempt to escape the *Titanic*. I hold her until she stops crying, then we drink the rest of the fairy wine and make fun of the movie until the world feels a little less heavy. At some point, Wren dozes off, and I'm left alone with my thoughts. Only the distant sound of city traffic and the ghosts of all the things I can't say out loud remain. I stare at my phone, wondering if André will come back. And a part of me wondering if I even want him to.

CHAPTER TEN

LIAM

"First rule," Todd says as he demonstrates, "always assume it's loaded. Keep your finger off the trigger until you're ready to shoot."

I nod, gripping the prop gun like it's made of glass. Erin stands nearby, arms crossed, her violet eyes sharp with scrutiny. She doesn't blink once. The gun looks too real to be a prop—cold, heavy, and realistic enough to make my palms sweat.

"Just relax, man," André calls, lounging against a set piece. "You've got this."

Todd runs through the blocking again, showing me how to wrestle the gun from André's hand before aiming and firing. It should've been simple. But my fingers feel like spaghetti—uncooperative and slick with sweat.

"Again," Erin says, her voice clipped.

Her gaze drills into me every time I fumble the grip. Todd stands beside her, ever patient, like I'm a toddler learning to walk. Technically, the gun only fires blanks, but they've made it clear that even a blank can do damage up close. Eventually, they give me the go-ahead to try firing.

"Just remember—don't point it at anyone. That's called flagging," Todd reminds me with a grin, a little too casual given the subject.

I take a breath and nod, adjusting my grip. Around us, the set hums with quiet activity—no glitches, no flickering lights, no technical problems. For once, everything feels normal... if you ignore the firearm in my hands. Todd fires a blank with a loud POP, smoke curling from the barrel. My turn. I lift the gun, trying to mimic him. Erin lets out a tired sigh.

"Trigger discipline," she snaps.

"Right. Trigger discipline." I adjust my finger, moving it off the trigger while trying not to shake.

We rehearse the scene again—André barges in, I grab the gun, aim low, and fire. A spark, a puff of smoke—my confidence grows.

"Just like that," Todd says.

Even Erin manages a half-smile.

"Don't get cocky," she warns.

But I can see it in her eyes—she's impressed. One more time. André lunges, we wrestle, I take the gun.

"Not bad, man," he says with a smirk. "You're a natural."

"Last time," Todd calls, grinning.

I grin back, distracted by Erin's smile as I reset my grip, aim, and—

Click.

Nothing.

I turn toward Todd. "Uh—"

"It's fine," he says. "Just set it down, and we'll—"

Before he can finish, the gun slips from my shaking hands and hits the floor, barrel up.

BANG.

Everything explodes into motion and stillness at the same time. Todd staggers back, clutching his neck as blood sprays—hot, coppery, wet—across both of us. Erin's scream splits the air, wild and raw. I want to move, but my legs refuse.

Someone shouts for a medic. Erin drops beside him, hands pressed to his neck.

"Somebody call 911!" she shrieks.

Her voice cracks—high and desperate—blood already soaking through her fingers. André bolts for help. I stand there, ears ringing, unable to tear my eyes away from Todd's gasping mouth and the widening pool of red beneath him.

"Liam!" Erin screams.

I fall to my knees beside them, trying to help, but my hands shake too much to do anything useful.

"Hang on, Todd. Please—just hold on!" she cries, rocking him against her. He grips her hand, eyes wide and terrified.

"I didn't mean to," I say. "I didn't mean to—"

Sirens in the distance.

Too far.

"Please, please," Erin whispers, tears streaking down her cheeks.

Paramedics burst onto the set and tear Todd from Erin's arms. I try to follow, but stumble, disoriented. Todd turns his head and grabs my wrist. His voice is wet, gurgling as his eyes meet mine.

"Get her out," he chokes, then goes limp.

"Losing him!" someone shouts as they rush out.

I stand there staring after them, covered in Todd's blood. Erin stands beside me, dazed, arms limp at her sides. I reach for her. She backs away.

"I can't—" Her voice cracks, and then she's gone, bolting off the set.

"Erin!" I yell.

André reaches for her, but she slips past—a streak of dark hair vanishing into the chaos. I race after her. Two crew members try to stop me. I shove past them and make it outside before André grabs my arm and pins me to the brick wall.

"Liam," he says firmly. "You need to stay."

Sirens scream onto the lot. Red and blue lights paint the asphalt.

A uniformed officer approaches, notebook in hand. "Sir, you need to remain here. We're going to need your statement."

I turn toward the gate, scanning for her.

"Where's Erin?" I ask, breathless. "Where did she go?"

"She's gone," André says quietly. "For now. But they'll find her. You stay. You help."

The officer flips open his notebook. "All right. Start from the beginning."

My limbs tremble as I take a breath.

"The set was quiet," I start, voice hoarse. "We were rehearsing with blanks. Todd was showing me how to handle the gun—he said it was safe."

The officer scribbles something down. "Were you aware that the prop gun had live ammunition?"

I blink, stunned. "No. No, it was supposed to be a prop. Just blanks. They triple-checked it."

André steps up beside me, nodding. "I thought we did."

The officer's eyes narrow. "So you're saying this was a mistake? That someone loaded the gun with a live round by accident?"

My stomach twists.

"I don't know. It—" I shake my head, remembering the sound. The spray. Todd's blood on my hands. "It wasn't supposed to happen."

The officer flips to a new page. "Did anyone on set have a reason to harm Mr. Wells or anyone else?"

The question catches me off guard.

"What?" I look at André, who looks just as shaken. "No. Why would—"

He doesn't answer. He doesn't have to. The question hangs there. *Not an accident.*

A possibility I hadn't dared to think of.

Until now.

—The set was swarming. Medics, crew, producers shouting over one another, trying to figure out who's in charge. But all I could see was Erin—her face frozen in shock, the blood on her hands. Todd's last words echoing in my ears—

Get her out.

Was he trying to protect her? From what?

The officer's voice breaks through again. "We'll need to collect the weapon and review footage from rehearsal. Can you provide a list of everyone who's had access to the props today?"

André jumps in, rattling off names. I stare down at my hands, still stained with dried blood, barely hearing him. My mind keeps circling back to Erin—how fast she'd run, how she hadn't looked back.

Is she hurt? Hiding? Wait... where's Claudia?

"Mr. Hartley?" the officer says again, pen hovering. "Is there anything else you want to tell us?"

I meet his gaze, my voice barely above a whisper. "Todd said something strange right before they took him away. He told me... to get her out."

The officer stiffens. "Get who out?"

I hesitate. "Erin."

He exchanges a glance with his partner. "Thank you. That's very helpful."

Helpful.

Like any of this felt helpful. Like any of this made sense. I turn away from the lights, from the cops, from André's hand still gripping my shoulder. I need to find her and figure this out. Before it's too late.

CHAPTER ELEVEN

ERIN

B *lood wouldn't stop. Blood wouldn't stop. Blood wouldn't stop. It* *wouldn't stop.*

Todd's neck—dark and gushing—pours a horrible red tide across the floor. My stomach turns, my eyes burn, and my skin goes cold. Everyone sees the same awful thing I see, but somehow they keep moving. Their screams ring in my ears while I stand there—unable to breathe, unable to do anything. The set crumbles into a blur of confusion, the ground pitching beneath me. My vision tunnels; blood is everywhere. Suddenly, it isn't just Todd. I see another body. Another victim. I hear a child's scream.

Claudia?

I stand there as they carry him away, gasping for air that won't come.

"Erin?" A voice cuts through the chaos, but I can't focus.

Can't see.

I'm drowning. Someone reaches toward me. I flinch and jerk away, the touch like fire on my skin. My limbs find motion on their own, and I scramble off the set, ignoring the blur of faces and voices as I bolt. My breaths come in ragged bursts. I push through doors, down hallways, my blood-stained hands leaving smears along the walls. I can't shake the feeling that more accidents are coming.

I'm dangerous.

"Erin, wait!" André's voice is close, but I don't stop.

I can't.

The need to escape—to outrun the image of Todd's neck gushing—pushes me faster, harder, away from everything. I catch a glimpse of Liam—wide-eyed, reaching out. But he's just like the rest—a smear in my periphery. I'm a ghost moving past him, past everything, until I reach my car and wrench the door open.

Tires screech as I speed out of the lot. Breathless, I drive, the city warping through my tears. Stoplights blur into streaks of red and green—the colors of Christmas and carnage. I don't slow until I'm blocks away, then pull off the main road into an abandoned parking lot.

Just me.

Just me alone in the car.

Just like I want.

The world buzzes outside my windows—impatient and alive. The air still smells like Todd's blood.

My phone vibrates against my thigh—sharp and jarring in the stillness. I almost ignore it—until the caller ID makes my stomach clench.

Nurse Sam—Mom.

"Hello?" My voice is barely there.

"Erin," Sam says, brisk but urgent. "It's your mother. You should come. Now."

The rest is muscle memory—keys in the ignition, hands on the wheel, the city blurring again. But this time, I'm not trying to escape. I'm racing toward something I can't stop.

The gates of the Cowles estate loom in the fog, iron-black against the pale sky. My fingers tremble as I punch in the code. The mansion rises ahead—grand, cold, and still. Inside, the halls echo with my footsteps, the air thick with the chill of death. Sam meets me at the door, her eyes widening at the sight of me, but she doesn't say a word as she leads me inside.

Mom's room is warm but dim, medical equipment humming softly beside the bed. She lies propped against pillows, her skin so pale it seems translucent. Sketchbooks, dried flowers, and photographs clutter the bedside table—fragments of a life that used to burn brighter.

"Mom," I whisper, moving to her side.

Her eyelids flutter. For a moment, I see her—really see her—the sharp wit and warmth I grew up with, even if it was always rationed. Her fingers curl weakly around mine.

"You came," she breathes.

Then her gaze shifts—just over my shoulder—and her lips twitch into something between recognition and surprise.

I glance back—the doorway is empty.

Sam moves quietly to the other side of the bed, checking the monitors.

"She wanted you to have this," Sam says, placing a small package in my palm.

"She said you'd know when you were ready to live your life without her," Sam adds softly before stepping out.

Something inside me splinters. I sink to my knees, clutching Mom's hand desperately, but the strength is already leaving her. Her breaths grow shallow as she watches me... then still. Always smiling.

The room feels too quiet. Too empty as tears streak down my cheeks.

I don't remember leaving—just the sound of my boots on marble, the package warm in my fist, the drive home a blur of headlights.

***

At home, I shove my dresser against my bedroom door. Then my bed. Anything to keep the world out. It's only then I notice—I'm still in the same clothes.

The blood is dried, stiff, and dark against my skin, crusted beneath my nails. The smell has turned sour. Without thinking, my disgust pulls me into the bathroom. I flip on the light and come face-to-face with my blood covered reflection. Shadows twist against the tile as if they're stuck there with me. I turn away just as I hear a snapping noise, followed by a crack.

I peel off my shirt but can't bear to look back. I already know what I'll see. Steam rises from the shower as I turn the handle, but when I reach to pull back the glass door, something snaps.

Glass.

A sharp crack splits the air, and the panel shatters, raining down in glinting shards. I flinch.

And then—

A memory.

—Claudia and I, years ago. Stockings. Firelight. My shadows lifting her higher, our laughter—and then flames. Pain. Smoke. Screams—

My knees buckle.

Not again.

The water streams behind me as I slump to the tile, my heartbeat thundering in my ears. I start to scream before bolting from the bathroom.

I curl up on the bedroom floor instead. The light from the bathroom still burns like hospital lights. I don't answer my phone. Let it buzz itself dead. Screen cracked.

Just like everything else.

***

I eat food I don't remember ordering as I wander my room. Clothes pile in a heap by the wall. Blood still crusts my hoodie. My skin itches, but I don't dare scratch. Somehow my bed ends up by the window, and my dresser lies in pieces against a wall.

Outside, the light changes.

Morning.

Afternoon.

Night.

Repeat.

The sky bleeds colors I stop recognizing.

Once, I reach for the door—only to shrink back from the handle as if it would burn me.

Then come the dreams. Todd's gurgling breaths. Claudia's screams. Claire's cold fury and the heat—*oh god, the heat*—across my back. I lie curled on the mattress, sheets tangled around my legs, the air still thick with the coppery scent of blood and sweat.

"Not again," I mutter.

Lamps shatter against the ceiling. Mirrors crack. Shadows flicker across the walls, slinking away every time I turn.

A knock. André and Wren. Voices at the door.

"Erin, we know you're in there."

I don't answer.

"The whole production is falling apart," André says. "People are saying the set is cursed."

I stay silent, curled up on the floor. Hair clings to my cheek.

"We're worried about you," Wren says. "Whatever happened with Todd wasn't your fault."

I wish I could believe her.

I hear them murmur, then retreat. I press my fists to my temples. Veins of shadow creep up my arms.

More memories spill in like poison:

—Claire dragging me down the stairs. "Do you think you're safe?" she spits. "Stay where you belong." Then fire. Poker. Screaming. "Erin!" Mom's voice. Hands pulling me out. Victor's voice. Confusion. Claudia—silent, watching—

When I come to again, I'm cold.

I blink against the light—real light.

Morning?

I don't know. My mouth is dry. The bed is stripped, the mattress bare. Dishes are piled on the dresser. A dried-up smoothie cup lies overturned by the door.

The bathroom door hangs ajar. I step inside without thinking and turn the knob.

The mirror is still shattered, but I can't remember when it happened. I blink at the web of cracks, my face fragmented and hollow.

Carefully, I scrape the glass aside with my foot as I step into the shower. I wince at the sting of water on my knees. Glancing down, I notice they're covered in blood with shards of glass.

When did that happen?

The water runs red, then pink, then clear. I scrub and scrub and still don't feel clean. I don't know how long I stand there. I only realize I'm crying when I choke on a sob.

Eventually, I stumble out and pull on my favorite gray hoodie, now covered in weird brown stains. In the pocket I find the package my mother left behind. Inside is her favorite silver locket with the inscription *kardia mu* on the back. I sit on the floor beside my bed and put the locket on, thumbing the worn inscription as I look around. The room is still in pieces. Shadows still linger. But something feels different...

I find my phone, dead and buried beneath a pile of dirty laundry. Plug it in. Let it buzz back to life. Dozens of missed calls. Messages. From André. From Wren. From Claudia.

And from Liam.

My hands shake as I hover over his name. Then I tap.

He picks up on the first ring. "Erin?"

His voice is breathless, like he can't believe I actually called.

I almost hang up. Almost let the silence swallow me. But I press the phone to my ear and close my eyes.

"Where are you?" he asks.

The question hangs between us. Tears slide silently down my cheeks as I curl up again on the floor, the phone pressed to my skin, his breathing the only thing grounding me.

I don't speak. Just listen. Just exist.

Let me stay like this, I think. *Please. Just like this.*

CHAPTER TWELVE

LIAM

The drone of the airplane engine fades beneath the echo of Erin's sobs looping in my mind. I've replayed that call so many times I can hear every breath, every choked cry, even now as I stare out the window at the endless stretch of sky.

Her voice had been raw and hoarse, and all I'd managed to ask was, "Where are you?"

I should've said more. Should've said anything. The flight attendant passes by again, offering a tight smile and a packet of salted almonds I didn't touch the first time. I nod out of politeness, or guilt, or habit—I don't know.

She stops two rows ahead, chatting with a man in a business suit. I catch the words "breaking news" and "so sad". Then she glances back toward me.

"Hey, aren't you from around Oakridge?" she asks, stepping closer, her phone already in hand.

My pulse kicks. "Yeah."

She tilts the screen so I can see. A news clip plays—Claudia in a dark dress, standing on the courthouse steps, microphones thrust toward her. The lower third reads: *Todd Wells Filming Tragedy—Safety Measures in Question.*

Claudia's voice is calm, her eyes red-rimmed but dry. "This is why we need stronger regulations on prop handling and firearm safety," she says. "No film crew should have to go through what we're going through."

The anchor's voice cuts in, summarizing "the accidental discharge of a prop weapon" and citing investigators who found "no evidence of foul play."

The flight attendant shakes her head. "Terrible, isn't it? Poor man. And she's so brave—coming out here to talk about it already."

I watch Claudia's lips move—the words neat and careful, the truth already scrubbed clean. Not a single mention of the bullet that shouldn't have been there.

"Yeah," I say finally, my voice flat. "Brave."

She smiles sympathetically and moves on, her phone still glowing in her hand. I stare at the seatback in front of me. My leg bounces restlessly under the tray table. The in-flight movie blinks on, some loud action flick with too much firepower and too little substance. Every explosion is a small reminder that my world has already gone up in flames.

Eventually, I have to move. I unbuckle my seatbelt and make my way down the narrow aisle to the bathroom, brushing past a guy with a neck pillow and earbuds. The second the door clicks shut behind me, I slump against it and dial.

The second ring doesn't even finish before André picks up. "Liam?"

"What the hell's going on?" I ask, my voice hoarse. "She called me. She sounded—André, she was crying."

"She hasn't left her room in days."

I grip the tiny sink, knuckles white. "Why didn't you tell me?"

"I didn't know it was this bad until a few days ago," he says. "We tried calling. Wren and I went over there. She wouldn't even open the door."

"I'm coming back," I say.

There's a pause.

"Just be careful. She's... Liam, she's really bad. She's not herself."

"Yeah," I mutter, ending the call.

My reflection in the mirror is a wreck—bloodshot eyes, five days past clean-shaven, haunted. I splash cold water on my face, hoping it might douse the panic. It doesn't. By the time I return to my seat, the movie is ending. I can't remember a single scene. But none of that matters. I'm going home.

***

LAX smells like jet fuel and disappointment. I shoulder my bag and push through the terminal, ignoring the ache in my legs and the heaviness settling behind my ribs. The carousel spits out my suitcase like an afterthought, and I haul it off with a grunt, dragging it through the throng of half-asleep travelers.

The Uber ride blurs past in city lights and suffocating silence. The driver eyes me in the mirror, probably wondering if I'm strung out. I don't have the energy to care. I stare out the window as familiar streets drift past, the glitter of Los Angeles colder than I've ever felt it.

By the time we pull up to Erin's house, it's past midnight. The porch light is off. Shadows pool at the edge of the driveway. I thank the driver out of habit and step into the dark. The front door sticks when I push it open. The air inside is quiet and still.

Too still.

I drop my bag by the entryway and freeze. Cushions lie scattered across the floor. A lamp lies shattered and tossed aside. And then there are the shadows.

They move—slithering, undulating, dancing across the walls and ceiling. They don't follow the light or seem to be cast by anything. They move on their own. They... watch.

My chest tightens. I pull out my phone, switch off airplane mode, and scroll through the unread messages. Erin's name fills the screen—frantic messages, cut off and unfinished.

Erin: *Liam, please!*

Erin: *I can't stop it.*

Erin: *I think I'm*

Nothing after that. André's messages are worse.

André: *She hasn't come out.*

André: *Something's wrong with Erin.*

André: *We need you. Please. Just come back.*

A surge of dread pulls me down the hall.

"Erin!" I shout, pounding on her bedroom door. "Erin, it's me!"

The handle won't budge.

Locked.

I slam my fist against the wood again. "Open up! Please!"

The shadows thicken around me, swirling in the corners like smoke rising from a funeral pyre. A chair lifts a few inches off the ground, then drops with a thud. My stomach drops with it.

Earthquake?

No.

No way.

I press my forehead against the door, whispering now. "Erin, I'm here. Please... just let me in. I'm not leaving."

The house creaks. The shadows pulse and begin to creep toward me. I back away, my throat tight. I don't know what this is. But I'm not going anywhere. I sink down with my back to the door, listening to the silence on the other side. After a few minutes, the shadows drift away.

Are they... are they alive?

I shake my head and close my eyes.

I must be losing it.

I take a deep breath and wait. And wait. The silence drags on.

It doesn't take long for me to lose track of time, my back pressed against the door. Then I start pacing, wearing a path into the hardwood outside her room. Each time I stop, I swear I hear her breathing just beyond the wall—or maybe it's just the house settling. This isn't worry anymore. This is fear. I stop in front of her door one last time.

"I'm sorry," I say—and mean it.

For everything. For leaving. For not realizing how bad it had gotten. For not knowing what the hell I'm walking into. Then I draw back my foot and kick the door with everything I have.

It splinters on impact, the frame cracking loud enough to echo down the hall. The lock gives way, and the door flies inward. There she is.

Erin.

She's curled up on the bed, still wearing the same hoodie she'd had on the last time I saw her—Todd's blood dried into the fabric, shadows coiling around her like snakes. Her eyes are huge and wild, locked on me like I'm the monster in the doorway.

"Erin!" I rush forward—

The shadows explode.

They erupt from every surface—walls, ceiling, floor—rushing toward me. They wrap around my arms and throat, tightening like they want to crush the breath from my lungs. I hit the floor hard, clawing at nothing, fighting for air. Everything is cold and wrong and swallowing me whole.

"STOP!" Erin's scream tears through the room.

And then—nothing.

The shadows recoil, leaving only a whisper of air in their wake. I lie there, gasping, staring up at her. She's standing now, trembling, tears streaming down her face, her expression twisted in horror.

"I didn't mean to—" she chokes out, backing against the wall. "I didn't mean to hurt you. Please. Just go. Please."

Her voice cracks on the last word, and my heart cracks with it.

"I can't control it," she whispers, sinking to her knees. "I don't want to hurt anyone else."

I push myself to my feet, still struggling to catch my breath. Then I cross the room in a few careful steps and drop to my knees in front of her.

"I'm not going anywhere," I say, my voice hoarse.

She shakes her head and pushes at me, her hands trembling and weak against my chest.

"Don't," she sobs. "Don't say that."

But I do.

Again and again, I whisper, "I'm not going anywhere."

Her hands go still. Then she collapses into me. Her body curls into mine, her head tucked under my chin like she's trying to disappear. And I hold her.

God, I hold her.

Then she starts to wail—sobs that shake her whole frame. Her tears soak through my shirt. Her fingers clutch me like I'm the only thing anchoring her to this world. And maybe I am.

"I've got you," I whisper.

"I can't do this anymore," she whispers in between waves of grief.

"You don't have to," I say softly. "I'm here."

Her breathing slows, and her body slumps heavier in my arms. We slide down to the floor together, still clinging to each other. I brush the hair from her face. She looks exhausted, and the shadows have retreated. The room is still.

She opens her eyes and looks at me, glassy and red. "Why?"

I don't answer. I just pull her closer. She doesn't push me away this time. So we stay like that—wrapped in silence, wrapped in each other. My mind races with questions—questions that have no answers. Not yet.

What was this?

What was she?

What were we?

But right now, none of that matters. Right now, I have her. And I'm not letting go.

CHAPTER THIRTEEN

ERIN

I'm a monster. There's no other way to see it.

Liam's hand cradles my face, wiping away my tears like it's the most natural thing in the world. Like I'm something fragile and human—anything but the abomination I know I am.

"Erin," His voice is soft, careful.

But his voice feels distant—buried beneath the roar of my own thoughts. His thumb brushes my cheek—and that's when I see it.

Blood.

Thick and red, seeping from the torn stitches across his palm. Each drop is a sickly-sweet reminder of—who and what—I am. Before I can even register what I'm doing, it's in my mouth. Copper floods my tongue, laced with a rush of bliss and ecstasy. I don't even realize I've moved until his skin is already against my lips. Until I see his eyes—wide with...

Horror.

And then it slams into me.

I jerk back, a fresh wave of tears blurring my vision.

"Liam." My voice breaks into a choked whisper. "I—"

I fed on him.

Like a goddamn leech.

I shake as I stare at the blood on my hands, on my skin—at what I've done.

He's exposed now.

A human tainted by the immortal world... and by me.

And it's all my fault.

All my fault.

My breathing turns ragged, chest tightening with rising panic. I stumble backward, knocking over a lamp, then a chair. My existence breaks everything—furniture, rules... and people.

"Erin, wait—!"

But I'm already running. My legs move on instinct, carrying me out of the room, through the house, and straight into the wet, black night. Rain lashes my skin, every drop sharp with shame. I run. I run before I can hear anything else.

Before my own thoughts can catch up.

I'm a blur—nothing but a desperate smear fleeing the blood, the horror, the truth. If I run fast enough, maybe it won't be real. Maybe I won't be real.

This is it.

This is the moment I've always feared—when everything finally falls apart and collapses around me. I've broken every rule.

Fed from him. Exposed him. Attached myself to him.

My bare feet pound the driveway. I don't feel the concrete or the gravel biting into my soles. Nothing can hurt as much as this. Nothing could ever hurt as much as facing him now—facing any of it.

My lungs burn as I reach the street, my muscles screaming with every step. The rain swallows me whole. It soaks through my hair, plastering my clothes to my skin. Each drop is a stinging reminder of how pathetic and lost I am. The pavement is slick beneath me, and I slip on the sidewalk, catching myself just in time.

"Erin!" Liam's voice cuts through the storm—closer than I expect.

I scream over my shoulder, "Leave me alone, Liam! It's too dangerous!"

My feet slap the pavement. Sharp pain shoots through my leg as I step on something, but I don't stop. I can't.

"Erin!" he shouts again—and I know he'll catch me.

He always does. His hand catches my arm, spinning me around. Suddenly I'm face-to-face with him, rain pouring down his cheeks. His eyes lock on mine.

"I don't care—I love you!" The words stun me.

So does the slick ground beneath us. My foot slips, and I lose my balance again. But Liam's arm shoots out, catching me before I hit the ground. He holds me there—soaked to the bone, shirt clinging to his chest, hair plastered to his forehead. I try to push him away—weakly, furious, frightened, trembling.

"You're an idiot!" I shout, the words half-lost in the rain. "Why are you being so fucking stubborn?"

He doesn't answer. Not with words. Instead, he pulls me close and kisses me—hard. His lips are warm against the chill of the downpour, and I drown in him. It feels like months of tension melt away—washed clean in that one explosive moment. I gasp against his mouth as he pulls back—breathless and wide-eyed.

"I learned from the best," he says, a wry smile tugging at the corner of his lips.

Then he kisses me again—deeper this time. Like he means it. Like he's trying to pour every ounce of love and recklessness into me. I wrap my arms around his neck, holding onto him like he's the only thing tethering me to the earth. And just when I thought maybe—maybe—I could stay in this moment forever—

Click.

The unmistakable click of a camera cuts through the haze. Liam pulls away. I stiffen in his arms, panic blooming sharp and fast in my chest. Someone is watching. But he doesn't let me go.

Instead, he sweeps me up into his arms before I can say a word. I clutch him, afraid—not of him, but of everything else. He carries me back toward the house, both of us drenched and breathless. I want to scream at him. To tell him to stop. To put me down. To run before everything gets worse.

But I don't. Because for the first time in forever, things don't feel broken beyond repair. They feel terrifying. And real. And even as the rain softens to a mist, I hold on to him. I hold on like my life depends on it.

Chapter Fourteen

Liam

Morning light filters through the sheer curtains, painting soft gold across Erin's face. Her hair has gone completely feral overnight—a wild halo of black against the pillow, making her look like some unholy mix between a rockstar and a goddess. I lean back against the headboard, arms folded behind my head, and just watch her breathe. There's a peacefulness to her sleep—real, solid peace.

The kind that makes my chest ache with how rare it is. After everything we've been through, this quiet feels like a miracle. It's hard to believe that just last night we were tangled in rain, panic, and kisses that tasted like relief. Now the chaos has condensed into something soft and fleeting—resting between us in the stillness of morning.

I nudge her shoulder. "Hey, bedhead."

She lets out a sleepy groan and rolls over, yanking the blanket over her head.

"Come on, Sleeping Beauty," I say with a grin. "The world awaits."

A single violet eye peeks out from beneath the blanket, narrowing into a deadly glare.

"Coffee," she croaks.

The demand is non-negotiable. She drags herself out of bed with the grace of a zombie, tripping over the tangle of blankets that trying to cling to her ankles. I follow her into the kitchen, watching her shuffle toward the coffee machine like it's her only salvation.

"You look great," I say, biting back a laugh. "Really put together."

Erin shoots me a look that could burn a hole through drywall. But then her expression softens, sleep still tugging at her edges. Then she gives me a slow, sleepy smile. I watch her lean against the counter as the machine sputters to life, the smell of coffee slowly reclaiming the room.

My phone lights up on the counter with a flurry of notifications. Expecting texts from André or Wren, I pick it up—then freeze.

Tabloid headlines scream from the screen: ***HARTLEY A HOME-WRECKER?,*** and ***ERIN CAUGHT CHEATING ON ANDRÉ?***

The accompanying photos are grainy and dark—but unmistakable.

Us.

Rain-drenched, clinging to each other like a goddamn Nicholas Sparks movie. My stomach drops. I turn the phone toward her. "Looks like we're famous."

She pales. I watch the blood drain from her face as she sinks into one of the kitchen chairs, her coffee forgotten in her hand.

"I knew this would happen," she whispers.

Her voice cracks with something deeper than fear—

Dread, maybe?

"I should've been more careful. This is bad, Liam. Really bad."

I try to shrug it off, keep things light. "Hey, it's just gossip. It'll blow over."

But her expression stops me cold. Her eyes go wide. The tremble in her hands makes the coffee ripple in her mug.

"You don't understand," she says. "This isn't just about the tabloids."

I frown. "Then what's it about?"

Erin inhales slowly, as if bracing. "It's about my family. My world."

I blink.

She meets my gaze. "I'm not like you. I'm not even human."

I stare at her, blinking stupidly. "You're... not human?"

Erin gives a shaky laugh that doesn't reach her eyes. "Surprise?"

I set my coffee down slowly, like any sudden movement might shatter the moment—or the universe itself. She straightens, like she's pulling strength from somewhere deep inside herself.

"My father is a vampire," she says quietly. "My mother's a water nymph."

I let out a breath I didn't realize I'd been holding. "You're serious."

She nods. "I can do things—things normal people can't. And there are rules, Liam. Ancient rules. Ones we've already broken just by—" Her voice catches. "Just by being together."

I can't stop staring at her.

She's still Erin.

Still the same woman who drinks coffee and smiles at me like I'm something worth believing in. But now there's this whole other layer—one filled with vampires and fae and rules I didn't even know existed. I suddenly think back to last night—to the shadows that attacked me, but stopped the second she screamed.

Can she... control shadows?

Erin reaches for me. "This is why I didn't want to get involved. If the Council finds out... they'll come after you."

My head starts to spin, and I take a deep breath. "Wait. A Council?"

Her nod is slow, reluctant. "They enforce the laws of the immortal world—vampires, fae, all of them. They don't care if you're innocent. Only that you're mortal. They'll see you as a threat."

I swallow hard and try to force the fear down.

Focus.

"What kind of laws are we talking about here?"

"The kind where we don't get a trial," she says. "The kind where they kill first and justify it later."

I lean forward, elbows on my knees, trying to make sense of everything I've just learned. "So your parents... they were breaking the rules too?"

Erin hesitates. "Victor—my father—was part of a powerful vampire family. Vera—my mother—was from the lower ranks of the water fae. They were childhood sweethearts, but when they got older, he was forced into an arranged marriage with someone else."

"Claire," I say, the name coming back to me from various meetings and scattered news articles.

She nods. "He married her, like the Council demanded—but only after they had me. I was born during his engagement to Claire."

My eyes widen. "And that was... forbidden?"

Erin gives a humorless smile. "Punishable by death. But Victor had power. He used it to protect her—stopped the execution. But he couldn't save her completely. They stripped her of her magic. Her glamour. Left her to fade."

"And now she's dying," I say softly.

Her voice wavers, but she doesn't look away. "She's already gone, Liam."

I freeze. "Gone?"

Erin's hand drifts to her collarbone, fingers curling around something beneath her shirt. She pulls out a delicate antique locket—silver, worn smooth from years of touch. "The nurse gave me this just before... before she passed. She said Mom wanted me to have it when I was ready to live my life without her."

I swallow hard. "Erin..."

Her eyes shine, but no tears fall. "I don't even know if I'm ready."

I step closer, sliding my hand over hers, feeling the faint tremble beneath my palm.

"And the worst part is... she chose this fate so she could have me," she murmurs.

I can't respond right away. I close my eyes and wrap my arms around her, my mind racing as I try to process everything. It's chaos and terrifying, but this is her world.

"Do you still want this?" she asks suddenly, her voice raw. "Do you still want... me?"

I open my eyes and look directly into hers. She looks so small then—not because of her size, but because of the way she folds in on herself, waiting for rejection like it was inevitable. And that's when I knew.

I knew I couldn't walk away. I truly, deeply loved her—more than my own life. I reach over and brush her hair gently behind her ear. Her eyes lock with mine—wide, violet, and filled with a terrible kind of hope.

"I do," I say simply.

She exhales like she's been holding that breath for years.

Then, maybe to escape the weight of everything, she murmurs, "Help me find a picture of her? I don't... I don't want to forget."

We end up on the floor in front of an open storage bin, the faint smell of jasmine rising from its contents. Old scarves. Stacks of brittle programs from long-forgotten art shows. Yellowed sketch paper.

I lift a heavy leather-bound book from the bottom. "This hers?"

Erin's eyes widen. "That's Mom's sketchbook." She flips it open, and I'm hit with page after page of delicate, haunting charcoal portraits—waves breaking against stone, faces lit by candlelight, a young Erin cradled in Vera's arms.

Tucked between the pages is an old photograph and a folded letter. The photo is of Vera—radiant, smiling—and a man I barely recognize: tall, silver-haired, with his arm around her shoulders.

The letter is addressed in precise script: *For Vera.*

I glance at Erin for permission. She nods.

Inside, the words spill out in a hand that's equal parts elegance and restraint:

> *You will always be the one I love.*
> *But I will step aside so you can*
> *have the life you've chosen. I pray*
> *Victor makes you happy. If he*
> *doesn't, know that I would have.*
> *—Lysander.*

Erin's breath catches. "Lysander... they were together?"

"It sounds like it," I say quietly.

She stares at the photograph as though seeing her mother for the first time—not just as "Mom," but as a woman with her own dreams and heartbreak. "He's been watching over me for years," she whispers. "No wonder he hates Claudia. No wonder he's... like that with me."

She flips through more pages, finding gallery stamps and award ribbons pressed flat between the drawings. "She was famous," Erin murmurs. "She gave it all up—her career, her magic—just to have me."

I rest my hand over hers, grounding her. "She didn't just give it up. She chose you."

For a long moment, we sit there in the dim light, surrounded by her mother's art. Then my phone buzzes violently on the counter. I pick it up, bracing for more headlines—but it isn't the tabloids this time.

André: *We need to talk. Meet me at this café.*

An address follows.

Downtown.

I turn the screen toward Erin. "Looks like André wants to meet up."

Her expression shifts, tightening with something between guilt and concern.

"He can help you understand," she says. "But be careful, okay?"

I try to muster some bravado.

"Don't worry," I say, grabbing my keys. "I can handle a coffee date."

"Promise me you'll listen to him."

I pause in the doorway. "I promise."

Outside, the world looks wrong—too sunny, too bright. Everything moves too fast, like I'm walking through a dream that hasn't caught up with reality yet. Traffic roars, pedestrians bustle past, and somehow none of it touches me. My thoughts are spinning.

Vampire. Nymph. Council. Death.

Erin.

The café André chose sits between a bookstore and a florist, all ironwork and ivy on the outside. Inside, it's cooler. Dimly lit. Soft jazz plays in the background. André's already there, seated in the back, hands folded around a ceramic mug. He raises a hand in greeting when he sees me.

"Liam," he says as I slide into the seat across from him. "Thanks for meeting on such short notice."

I shrug, trying to play it cool.

"Figured we should sort out our 'love triangle,'" I say, making air quotes.

André smirks faintly. "Yes, about that. I wanted to make a few things clear."

"Erin already told me everything," I cut in. "About the Council. About you."

He doesn't flinch—just nods, slowly.

"Then you understand this isn't a rivalry. I care for Erin—deeply—but she's never returned those feelings." There's no bitterness in his voice.

Just a quiet kind of sadness.

"I had to decide," he continues, "whether to walk away or stay in her life as a friend. I chose to stay."

I shift in my seat. "And you're okay with... this? With me?"

André's gaze stays level as he talks. "It's what she wants. And I want her to be happy."

He takes a slow sip of his drink. "But you should know what you're stepping into."

"I'm starting to get the idea," I mutter.

"The Council won't be merciful," he says. "They'll see you as a liability. A threat. Erin's already on thin ice because of her bloodline."

I frown. "Because of her parents?"

André nods. "Victor and Vera broke a fundamental law. He was a high-ranking vampire; she was middle-class fae. Their affair destroyed two arranged alliances. The Council considered it treason. Erin's birth was a scandal—half-blood, illegitimate, powerful. They wanted her dead from the start."

My stomach twists. "What happened?"

"Victor used every ounce of his influence to protect them," André says. "He kept his marriage to Claire to appease the Council. But Vera was punished. Her glamor and magic were stripped. She's been dying ever since."

"And now Erin's repeating the same mistake," I say quietly.

"Yes and no. She's not her mother," André reminds me. "She's something new. Stronger. But that means she's even more dangerous in the Council's eyes. And you're not exactly from our world—you're an even greater taboo."

I take a slow breath, trying to steady the chaos inside me. "Then what do I do?"

André tilts his head. "You decide if it's worth it."

I meet his gaze. "It is. I want her—no matter what comes with it."

For the first time today, André smiles—really smiles.

"Then be ready," he says. "Because they're coming."

CHAPTER FIFTEEN

ERIN

I guess there are worse ways to die than with a hangover, but right now I can't think of any. I cradle my mug of black coffee like it's the only friend I have left in the world and stare down at the headline screaming in bold type: ***HOLLYWOOD'S HOTTEST NEW COUPLE!***

My face—locked in a rain-soaked kiss with Liam—stares back at me from the front page. Even in my current state, I have to admit—we look good.

The phone buzzes again, rattling across the counter. The name "Victor" flashes on the screen. Third message. The urgency practically oozes through the glass.

I groan and bury my face in my hands. Nothing like a summons from your father to set the tone for the day. Of course, I should've seen this coming. Cowles family meetings never mean anything good. And somehow, I'm always in trouble.

The drive to the estate is a blur of anxiety and palm trees. My knuckles go white on the steering wheel as I rehearse excuses that won't work.

Maybe I'll say it was all a PR stunt?

Or that I was drunk and confused?

But I already know Victor would see right through the lies.

The massive iron gates loom ahead. My stomach twists tighter with every turn up the winding road.

The mansion's opulent marble foyer feels more like a cave than a home. Claire's frosty perfume hangs in the air. I pause, trying to steel myself for the inevitable lecture. Then I head inside.

Victor is waiting, posture stiff, concern and disappointment carved in equal measure across his face. He ushers me into his study—a shrine to his ego. Leather-bound books, a glinting whiskey decanter, and framed posters from his Oscar-nominated films decorate the room.

Claire's already there, pacing in her designer heels. Her eyes meet mine, and her face twists into a scowl. Victor slides printouts across the desk—tabloid screenshots with headlines in red font: ***SECRET AFFAIR? HOLLYWOOD LOVE TRIANGLE EXPOSED!***

"The Elders are in an uproar," he says. "These photos are everywhere, Erin."

"And whose fault is that?" Claire snaps. "Do you have any idea what you've done?"

I flinch.

"Generations of secrecy—risked because you couldn't control yourself with some human actor," she spits. "You've jeopardized everything."

"I didn't mean for this to happen," I say quietly. "I love him."

Claire practically chokes on the word. "Love," she scoffs. "How quaint. And how utterly reckless."

Victor studies me, his eyes softer than hers but heavy with judgment.

"You need to understand how serious this is," he says. "Certain factions are already calling for Liam's execution."

He pauses. "And possibly yours."

The words send a chill down my spine, but I'd anticipated this. Interracial relationships were taboo, and relationships with mortals even more so.

"I'm aware," I reply.

Victor nods grimly. "End it. Publicly. Immediately. Or face the consequences."

I squeeze my eyes shut, fighting the urge to scream at him. My whole life, I've followed this family blindly, desperately trying to be the perfect daughter. Desperately trying to measure up to their expectations.

I'm supposed to obey, aren't I?

To be a good daughter?

But when I reach for home—for warmth, for love—I find Liam. My mother's dying face flashes in my mind.

Could I be like my father?

I think of Liam's fate—how he'll be strung along, drugged up, and treated like a toy. Then, when he's of no further use, he'll be just another "celebrity overdose" on the news.

Is it worth it?

I remember the way Liam held me the other night, the way his lips felt against mine, the way he smiles when he looks into my eyes. And in that moment, I know. I'm not my father's daughter. I stand slowly, tears slipping down my cheeks. My voice is calm and firm when I look my father in the eye.

"I choose him," I say. "Even if it means we both will die."

Victor's eyes widen, and for a moment, the mask of duty slips.

He looks... caring.

Like the man who'd once steadied my handlebars when he taught me to ride a bike without falling. He comes around the desk and grips my shoulders with surprising warmth.

"If this is truly your choice," he whispers, "don't look back. Don't hold back like I did."

His voice cracks. "If anyone can change their fate, it's you. Be strong where I was weak."

I blink at him, stunned. The Victor Cowles I know doesn't offer advice—he gives ultimatums. Yet here he is, telling me to be better—to follow my heart. I nod, swallowing the lump in my throat as I turn toward the door.

Claire's voice hisses behind me. "You selfish girl! You'll get us all killed!" Her heels strike the floor like gunshots as she follows me out. "Don't you dare walk away like your life is the only one that matters!" It doesn't hit the way it used to.

Not anymore.

I pause at the threshold—not for her, but for myself. Remembering all the years I fought for her approval. For their approval. Then I walk out. I don't slam the door or run. I just leave it all behind. Outside, the afternoon sun is sharp and alive.

No more shadows. No more hiding. For the first time in days, I can breathe.

My phone buzzes in my pocket. I pull it out and glance at the screen.

Nathan: *Claudia's planning something dangerous. Call me ASAP!*

My chest tightens.

Of course she is.

Sliding into my car, I stare at the long driveway ahead. Exhausted, but the warmth of Victor's words still hums in my chest. The only other time I've felt this warmth is with Liam.

Is this what love is supposed to feel like?

I grip the wheel and inhale slowly. The only world I've ever known is unraveling, thread by thread—but I'm not scared anymore. Not afraid to break rules or shatter expectations. Power rises in my veins—like something long buried finally waking. Shadows coil around my fingertips—obedient now. Responsive.

They bloom in my palms like dark wildflowers—alive with purpose. I start my engine, my path uncharted but mine alone. I guess it's true—I'm not my father's daughter. I never truly was.

Chapter Sixteen

Liam

For the first time in days, I'm starting to think I might actually be okay. Sure, I'm in way over my head—the whole immortal world thing is a lot—but Erin is real. That much I know. That much I trust.

I step out of the café and blink into the afternoon sun, it's warmth hitting me like I've just been reborn. A fragile calm settles over me.

Maybe the worst is over. Maybe Erin and I could actually—

A white van screeches to a stop barely three feet in front of me. I don't even finish the thought before rough hands are on me—grabbing, dragging, wrenching me off my feet. I try to shout, but a hood slams over my head, plunging me into darkness. I kick out blindly—my foot connects with nothing but air.

The van jerks into motion, the floor tilting hard enough to throw me sideways. I thrash and fight, but panic hits fast and hot, squeezing the air out of my lungs. For a second, I'm sure I'm going to pass out. Then—just as abruptly—the van slams to a stop. The back doors burst open with a metallic crack, and hands drag me by the hood. Someone rips it off so hard that I nearly topple backward—only for my legs to be kicked out from under me. My head smacks on something hard.

Blackness.

Cold water shocks me awake, pouring over my scalp and down my spine.

Harsh overhead light floods my vision, revealing cold concrete, cavernous echoes, and the steady drip of water somewhere out of sight.

A warehouse. Of course.

And I'm tied to a chair—ropes biting so deep into my wrists it feels like their carving me open.

So much for "being okay".

Footsteps—measured, sharp, purposeful—echo through the silence. Claudia emerges from the shadows, smiling ear to ear like she's walking onto a red carpet instead of a crime scene. Her golden hair glints under the single swinging bulb like she's posing for it. Her red eyes lock onto mine, pinning me in place. Behind her, several robed figures materialize—tall, silent, draped in heavy black.

The Elders. Fantastic.

They watch me like I'm a rabid animal they finally managed to corner. Claudia circles me, her heels clicking out a sharp staccato rhythm on the concrete.

"You've been a hard man to kill, Liam," she says—eerily cheerful, like she's praising a pet. "That railing on set... the prop gun that 'misfired' on poor Todd..."

My stomach drops, all the blood draining from my face at once.

"Why?" I croak, throat sand-dry.

She pauses. For a moment, something cracks through her perfect composure—something sharp and vicious.

Something ugly.

"I brought you into Erin's life to hurt her," she says, smiling like she's discussing the weather. "You weren't supposed to matter. But then... you did.

The Elders drift forward, silently. One of them speaks in a voice that sounds like gravel being ground under a boot—low, ancient, final. "His knowledge endangers our world. The mortal must be eliminated."

I yank against the ropes, panic sharpening every breath. "I won't tell anyone—I'll disappear, whatever you want. Just don't do this."

Claudia laughs—a sharp, unhinged sound that echoes off the walls. "Still so naïve," she purrs. "Even now."

Cold fear punches through my ribs, knocking the air out of me.

"What about Erin?" My voice cracks open. "Is she safe?"

Claudia leans in until her breath ghosts across my cheek. Her perfume wraps around me—a sweet vanilla with a rotten edge, suffocating.

"Don't worry about Erin," she whispers. "Worry about how little time you have left."

Her smile stretches unnaturally, canines lengthening just enough to send my heart into overdrive—her face twisting into something monstrous and delighted. She blows me a kiss—mocking, taunting—then turns on her heel, hips swinging with cruel confidence, that smile carved permanently onto her face.

"I never intended for you to leave here alive." She calls back, her voice echoing long after her footsteps fade.

Now I'm alone.

Alone—with the Elders watching me like wolves deciding which part to eat first.

And waiting for whatever comes next.

CHAPTER SEVENTEEN

ERIN

My cell phone rings, and I already know. Even before I pick it up—before the static hiss hits my ear—the dread is already twisting in my gut. Claudia doesn't even bother with a hello.

"Tick-tock, big sister," she purrs. "You have one hour to retrieve your pet human, or I'll end him myself."

My heart stutters. "Liam…"

His name barely leaves my mouth before Claudia sighs theatrically.

"Such a fighter," she muses. "Even with his hands tied behind his back, he still thinks he stands a chance. Still thinks you'll come for him."

The room tilts—shadows slithering along the walls, responding to the fury pulsing through me.

I grip the phone tighter, knuckles whitening. "If you touch him—"

"Oh, Erin." Her giggle is sharp and manic. "I already have."

The line goes dead with a finality that cracks something deep inside me. I stand frozen, my phone cracking under the pressure of my grip. The air around me thickens, charged and vibrating. My breath goes shallow as a tremor ripples through the house.

Picture frames rattle on the walls. A vase tips off a nearby shelf and shatters. Lightbulbs flicker—then explode in a burst of white heat.

I don't care.

I stand in the chaos, trembling not with fear but with fury—pure, blood-boiling fury. "Fuck the rules. Fuck the Elders." My voice cracks with rage. "Fuck Claudia." I grab my jacket, the fabric buzzing where it brushes my arms. Shadows coil around my shoulders, drawn to the surge of power rippling through me. I catch my reflection in the hallway mirror—eyes almost black, only the faintest ring of violet clinging to the edges. A dark, humorless chuckle escapes my lips.

Let them see what I really am.

Let them try to stop me.

***

The night swallows me whole as I storm into the underground district—a secret artery beneath Los Angeles where the supernatural come to bleed and bargain. Neon signs flicker in every forbidden color. The air reeks of sweat, blood, and magic too old to be legal. No one dares to stop me. Whispers trail in my wake; shadows bend at my feet like loyal dogs. I don't bother hiding my powers.

Let them stare. Let them cower. Let them know.

Lysander's club rises from the street—slick, opulent, every surface dripping with sin. I don't even break stride as I shove past the bouncer. He doesn't try to raise a hand. Inside, music throbs and bodies grind against each other like animals in heat. Immortals sprawl across velvet lounges—drinks in one hand, prey in the other. At the far end, under a chandelier made of bones and starlight, Lysander reclines in his private booth. He's surrounded by a constellation of beautiful people—polished teeth, hollow eyes. But when he sees me, his smile sharpens.

"Erin," he drawls, voice velvety and sharp. "To what do I owe the pleasure?"

I don't bother with pleasantries. "Liam's been taken. Tell me where he is."

He leans forward, interest sharpening. "Ah. The human."

Shadows curl tighter around my legs as I step closer. "This isn't a request."

Lysander's eyes gleam. "What's in it for me?"

I meet his gaze without blinking. "How about the heads of all the Elders?"

Silence snaps across the club. Conversations die mid-sentence. Glasses freeze mid-air. Every immortal within earshot turns to look. Lysander's pupils dilate, just slightly.

He studies me for a long moment, then breaks into a slow, hungry grin. "Well," he purrs. "Now you have my attention."

He flicks a finger at one of his lackeys—a pale slip of a fae clutching a clipboard. The boy rushes forward, thrusting a paper and pen into his hand.

Lysander scribbles something quickly, then hands the note to me. "Word is they're holding him here. But you know how rumors can be."

I glance at the coordinates. My heart stutters.

"I'm getting Liam back," I say, "or I'll burn the world down trying."

Lysander chuckles, reclining again. "Your mother would be proud."

My phone buzzes as I turn to leave.

I don't check the cracked screen—I just answer.

"Will my services be required?" Morana's voice oozes through the speaker.

"Meet me at Lysander's coordinates," I reply, grinning as I hang up.

***

Outside, the air pulses with electricity. I move like lightning down the street, adrenaline and fury fueling every step. Streetlamps burst overhead, glass raining down like glitter. Shadows lick at my heels. A man drops his drink when the ice flash-freezes in his glass. My fingertips spark with coiling darkness, power singing hot in my veins.

"Erin!" Wren's voice cuts through the storm.

I turn, wild and breathless, as she sprints toward me. André's just behind her, his expression tight with concern. Wren's curls bounce as she catches up, her eyes wide.

"We got your message," she says, breathless. "Are you okay?"

I look away. "They took Liam."

André looks at me the way someone might look at a lit fuse. "Shit... Do you need help?"

"I'm not sure," I say, showing them the coordinates. "We have a location."

Wren grabs my wrist, her touch grounding. "Do you have a plan?"

I blink and stare at the cracked asphalt beneath our feet.

"Find Liam. Kill Claudia. Burn the rest to the ground." A streetlight explodes behind me as I speak.

Both of them flinch. André exchanges a glance with Wren. "You know she's serious."

"Dead serious," I mutter, pulling away and striding down the road. "You coming or not?"

Wren rolls her eyes and follows. "Like we'd let you have all the fun."

The city blurs around us as we move—me in the lead, fury and vengeance propelling me forward. Wren and André flank me like shadows, our steps in sync as we cut through alleys and empty streets. My vision isn't just sharpened—it's altered. I can see traces of Liam's fear drifting through the air like smoke. I can taste it—iron and adrenaline.

We enter the industrial district as dusk slips into full night, every window going dark, every building a looming mausoleum of rust and rot. I stop outside a fenced-off loading dock. My skin prickles. A memory stirs—sharp and unwelcome.

"Wait," Wren whispers, grabbing my arm. A figure steps out from behind a row of stacked shipping containers, arms lifted in surrender.

"Before you shadow-stab me, I'm here to help." A soft voice calls out.

Calm, cocky—too familiar.

I freeze, fury crackling at my fingertips. "You?"

He takes another cautious step forward, hands still raised. "Me."

Wren blinks in confusion. "Nathan?"

André steps subtly in front of Wren.

I narrow my eyes, powers surging as shadows snake toward him. "You've been working with them this whole time?"

Nathan doesn't flinch. I fight against the shadows, struggling to rein them in.

Shadows dart around us, crackling like loose wires.

"With them. Against them. Only for you." His gaze locks with mine. "Who do you think gave Lysander these coordinates? I know where she's keeping him."

I don't move. "Why should I believe you?"

"Because I could've led you into a trap just now—and I didn't." He reaches into his pocket and pulls out a folded document, a receipt, and several photos.

"An old slaughterhouse." He explains, handing them to me. "Guard patrols. Old magic. Booby traps."

I scan the papers once, then hand them to Wren. "I'm going in."

Nathan's hand darts out, catching my wrist. "Wait—we need a plan."

"We don't," I snap, jerking my hand free.

Shadows flare outward like wings, answering the spike in my pulse. "I'm not slowing down."

"Erin, listen—if you charge in blind, you could—"

"Lose him?" My laugh cracks, bitter and wet. "I'm not losing anything."

Nathan exhales, exasperated. "Can you at least try to—"

"No." I turn to Wren and André. "Are you coming?"

"Mom's gonna kill me," Wren mutters, but she grins. "Hell yeah."

André shrugs with a resigned smile.

"Told you she wouldn't wait," he says, shooting Nathan a knowing look.

Wren gives Nathan an apologetic glance, then steps to my side. "She's made up her mind. Let's move."

Nathan drags a hand through his hair. "You're impossible."

"Then don't follow," I toss over my shoulder, already walking away.

But his footsteps fall in behind me anyway. "I'm coming!"

We reach the edge of the industrial district. The slaughterhouse looms ahead—an omen carved in rust and shadow. But for the first time, I'm not afraid of dying. I can feel Liam's presence—close, faint, terrified—and my pulse quickens with something wild and electric. Wards shimmer around the building, ancient and humming, making my skin prickle. Nathan catches up beside me, slightly breathless.

"Are you ready for this?" he asks between breaths.

I turn toward him, a reckless smile curving my lips. "I was born ready."

I can taste the moment—sweet, savage, inevitable. "I've been waiting my whole damn life to do this."

Chapter Eighteen

Liam

They say Hollywood is a cutthroat town, but I never thought they meant it so literally. The first thing I've learned about being kidnapped? It's boring as hell. The second is that boredom is a lot easier when you're not tied to a chair. The ropes gnaw at my wrists and ankles, every twitch a reminder that I'm way out of my depth.

The slaughterhouse is really more warehouse than fortress. And I swear the ghosts of a thousand dead cows are judging me while I wait for my own ass to get ground into hamburger.

"Your girlfriend's late, huh?" the guard says, hovering near the door, eyes flicking between me and his phone.

He looks about as dangerous as a wet sock, but I'm not stupid enough to test that theory. I shift, trying to find any position that doesn't make my hands go numb.

"Not her style to stand me up," I say. "Maybe she's just busy picking out a coffin for me."

He smirks, but his fingers won't stop fidgeting with the keys on his belt. He's been pacing for hours, wearing a groove into the concrete. *I can work with that.*

"You seem nervous," I say casually. "Second thought's about Claudia's orders?"

He freezes, eyes narrowing. "You don't know anything."

"True," I admit. "I'm just the pet human, right? But I'm guessing you didn't sign up for this."

He hesitates.

That's my opening.

"An acting coach once told me: if you're not feeling it, you're not doing it right."

"What do you know about feelings?" he snaps, but there's a crack in his voice now.

"I know you've got 'em. I can see it on your face." I lean back as far as the ropes allow. "You don't want to do this."

His gaze darts to the door and back.

"I didn't sign up to kill people," he mutters. "I just needed the money. I didn't think..."

"Join the club," I say dryly. "I'm tied to a chair."

He looks at me then—really looks—like he's seeing me for the first time. "You love her, don't you? Erin."

"More than my own life," I admit, and it terrifies me. "Not that it's worth much right now."

He shifts, conflict written all over him.

"There's a prophecy," he says, voice low. "About a child with vampire and fae blood. The Elders think it'll destroy them."

My stomach drops, pieces fitting together into a terrifying picture. "And Erin's the one they're afraid of."

My blood goes cold.

If they feared her—feared her enough to kill—then how much danger had I dragged into her life just by loving her?

"That's why Claudia—" He stops, shaking his head. "She's working with extremists. They think if the prophecy is fulfilled, the Elders will fall."

I let out a shaky breath. "And here I thought dating an actress would be less dramatic."

I meet his eyes, mustering every ounce of sincerity I have left. "You don't have to do this. Let me go."

He bites his lip. "If they find out—"

A crash echoes down the hall.

The guard jumps. I hear it too—distant shouts, boots pounding against concrete.

"Go," I urge. "Get out while you can."

He looks at me one last time, guilt etched into every line of his face—then bolts. The door slams behind him, and I yank at the ropes—fighting, swearing, desperate. The whole slaughterhouse vibrates with chaos.

"They're breaking through!"

"Get the Elders!"

"Erin!"

Her name jolts through me. I twist harder against the restraints. Skin tears, blood smears—but I don't care.

She's here.

She actually came.

I fight like hell, ropes digging deeper into raw flesh. The air crackles, and shadows slither across the walls like living smoke. Waves of shimmery force and sparks slam into the walls and windows.

"Focus!"

"Hold the line!"

Another crash—closer this time.

I hear them; see the shimmers, the sparks; feel the slaughterhouse shake with each blow.

"Come on, come on," I hiss, muscles screaming as I wrench one hand free.

The second rope snaps just as the door bursts open.

"Liam!" Erin stands in the doorway, eyes glowing violet and black, tendrils of shadow writhing around her like living flame.

"Erin!" I stagger to my feet, breath tearing from my lungs.

She runs to me, arms wrapping tight around my neck.

"I thought—" Her voice breaks. "I thought I was too late."

"Not even close." I manage, though my voice shakes.

She pulls back, searching my face with those wild, beautiful eyes—and I don't get the chance to say another word.

Movement flickers behind her.

Too fast to shout a warning.

"Erin, look out!" I shove her behind me—and pain explodes through my chest.

White-hot agony.

Blinding, obliterating everything else.

Something silver plunges in—deep—again and again. My knees buckle as I choke on the coppery taste of my own blood.

Claudia's voice tears through the haze—shrill, frantic. "No! It wasn't supposed to happen like this! You were just the bait!"

A silver dagger clatters to the floor as I sway, red blooming across my chest like spilled ink.

Erin catches me before I hit the concrete, holding me close, her face twisted with horror. "Liam! No, no, no—"

"I love you," I manage, blood bubbling between my lips.

"Stay with me." She bites into her wrist and presses the bleeding wound to my mouth. "Please—stay with me."

Her blood fills my mouth—burning, bittersweet. A desperate gamble. I try to drink.

To become like her. To survive.

I want to—God, I want to.

But I'm slipping. Too fast.

"Don't leave me," she whispers, a tear striking my cheek like a spark. "Don't you dare leave me."

I manage a faint smile up at her.

At least I can die knowing she's okay, I think, clinging to her voice as the world narrows—then goes black.

CHAPTER NINETEEN

ERIN

He's gone... He's gone, and we almost made it...

The thought's a jagged scream in my mind as I cradle Liam's body, his blood warm and sticky on my hands. The world around me blurs—shadows tremble, cold concrete biting into my knees—but I kneel there, frozen in shock. He died saving me. The horror of it hollows me out completely.

"Liam," I croak.

The sound of his name barely forms in my throat. The warehouse has gone unnervingly still. The chaos of moments ago dissolves into silence. I can still feel his warmth—the last trace of life slipping away. A sob claws its way up my chest, and I choke on the sound.

"Oh, Erin," Claudia mocks from behind me. "I warned you this would happen."

I look up, too numb to register reality, and see her step forward with a smile sharp enough to curdle blood.

"Did you really think we'd let you keep your human pet?" she taunts, circling us like a vulture.

My heart twists. The grief inside doesn't break me—it mutates, twisting into something sharp and furious. My body trembles—not from grief, but from something far darker. Rage, pure and unrelenting, coils through me as Claudia's laughter ricochets off the walls.

The shadows respond before I do—writhing, coiling, alive.

"Poor big sister," Claudia purrs. "Losing him twice must really hurt."

I move without thinking—faster than I ever have in my life. Claudia's eyes widen in shock as I lunge at her. My hand locks around her throat, lifting her clean off the ground.

"Erin!" she gasps, clawing at my wrist as her feet kick uselessly in the air.

I don't speak. I don't flinch. I don't feel anything at all. The shadows rise around me, thickening like smoke. Their edges sharpen, vibrating with hunger—then they descend.

She screams as the tendrils slither over her arms, face, and torso—slicing as they go. They peel her apart like fruit—slow, merciless—her blood spraying the air in a fine crimson mist. Her screams shatter the stillness—a sound too raw for even the Elders to ignore. They move at last.

One steps forward, robes billowing, hands rising to cast an ancient binding spell. Two others draw ceremonial daggers, shouting incantations in a language lost to time. The shadows don't need direction. They surge outward, slicing through flesh and bone like wet paper.

Blood sprays. Limbs fall. One of the Elders collapses, headless. Another screams as his legs separate from his torso. Even the most stalwart among them stumble back, slipping in gore as their fear fills the air. Their retreat is frantic—pathetic.

Intoxicating.

Claudia's shrieks shift—from rage, to fear, to pleading.

"Please!" she cries. "I'm your sister—have mercy!"

But I have no mercy left to give her. The shadows tighten around her, savoring every slash and tear. Her body comes apart in slow, gruesome ribbons. Her pride, her power—slowly torn away.

My grip never falters, even as her limbs hang useless and her mouth collapses into a torn, gore-slick maw. Everything they've stolen from me—everything they've dared to do—will be repaid in blood. Then, through the carnage, a voice cuts through.

"Erin?" I freeze.

My breath hitches—my fingers loosening. I turn. And there he is—exactly where I left him, slumped against the wall.

Liam.

My mind can't comprehend it—can't believe it.

It has to be a trick.

It has to be.

But his eyes are open.

Wide.

Alive.

His skin shimmers faintly—a ghost of luminescence across his pale chest. The wounds are gone. Faint scars remain, but no blood. He's breathing.

Breathing.

I drop Claudia like an afterthought.

She collapses, gasping, clutching her shredded throat as her body desperately tries to knit itself back together. Her cries grow distant—irrelevant—as the shadows slither back to me, curling protectively around my ankles as I cross the room. I drop to my knees beside him. He looks up at me like I'm the miracle.

"Erin," he breathes, voice fragile and full of wonder.

His eyes search mine as though seeing everything for the first time.

"You're okay," I whisper, my fingers brushing his cheek.

My hands tremble—bloody, shaking with disbelief. "You're okay."

A crooked smile tugs at his lips.

"I wouldn't say okay," he murmurs, glancing down at his chest.

The faint scars shine like silver thread stitched beneath his skin. "But definitely not dead."

The breath I hadn't realized I was holding rushes out of me. My tears come fast and hot as I lean forward and pull him into my arms. He winces—but then his arms come around me too. Wrapping around me, holding me like he'll never let go.

And maybe he won't have to—not anymore.

Chapter Twenty

Liam

T hey say your whole life flashes before your eyes when you
die—but they don't tell you how much faster it flashes when
you wake up again. Memories tear through me like a runaway train.

—My first guitar, Tally's birthday party, the time Mom caught me smoking out the window—

They crash into each other, a kaleidoscope of sights and sounds
that would've knocked me flat if I weren't already on the floor. I gasp.
The air is sharp, laced with scents I've never noticed before—oil,
rust, blood. Every heartbeat and breath around me hits like thun-
der—each one distinct, unbearably loud.

I squeeze my eyes shut as the world spins—then I see her.

Erin.

Even across the room, I see the way light dances along every strand
of her hair—the shimmer of her skin pulsing with something alive
and ancient. Her heartbeat cuts through the chaos—steady, familiar,
grounding. She's terrifyingly beautiful.

My center of gravity. My tether.

Then the thirst hits—a searing, unrelenting, stripping away
everything else. Panic claws up my throat. I clutch at my neck,
writhing as pain tears through my gums—fangs splitting through.

I have fangs.

They break through like splinters of bone. My head feels like it's splitting—a war between memory and instinct, humanity and hunger.

"Liam." Her voice slices through the haze.

I look up—wild, desperate, trembling. Erin kneels beside me, her hands finding mine. Her touch sends warmth spiraling through me.

"It's okay," she murmurs, her voice calm and certain in a way I can't begin to be. "You're okay."

I shake my head hard.

I'm not. I can't be.

The hunger is too loud, too hot. I try to speak, but no words come—only need. She seems to understand. Gently, she brings her wrist to my mouth.

"Drink," she whispers. "It's the only way."

I flinch.

I don't want to hurt her. Don't want to need this. But the fire inside me is swallowing everything. I hesitate—

Then I bite down. Her blood floods my mouth—thick, metallic, shockingly warm.

It's life. It's power. It's her.

The fire dims instantly, replaced by a rush that slams through me like lightning. My body trembles as the pain bleeds into something bright, electric, alive. Images burst behind my eyes.

—Mom's lullabies, the hum of traffic, the rasp of a cricket's wings, the city's neon heartbeat—

I cling to her wrist, overwhelmed, floating through a universe of sensation. Around us, voices rise—shouting, cursing.

"Abomination!"

"They broke the Law!"

"A prophecy fulfilled..."

I barely hear them. I pull back slowly, lips stained red, breath ragged. Erin cups my cheek, wiping the blood away with her thumb. Her touch is soft.

Certain.

Then she kisses me, and the world narrows to just the two of us.

I'm alive. Reborn. Hers.

"Liam," she breathes, smiling through tears.

I don't have the words.

Not yet. But I will.

"Ahem."

The sound snaps us apart. We turn to see Lysander and Morana standing at the edge of the wrecked slaughterhouse—both dressed like they've stepped off the set of an opera. Lysander's smirk deepens as he surveys the collapsed walls and the mutilated remains of several Elders.

"You two certainly had some fun, huh?" Morana chuckles as she picks up the decapitated head of an Elder and casually kicks it aside.

"You'll need to vanish. The remaining Elders, the extremists—even some of your own kind—will come for you." She glances toward Wren and André, who are busy corralling curious humans.

Lysander's voice takes on a theatrical lilt. "You'll have a target on your backs until the end of time. The prophecy, Liam's little rebirth, Erin's shadow-show... it's far too much for our society to stomach."

I look at Erin. Her eyes meet mine as she smiles. I feel it too—that heady, terrifying thrill of being unstoppable.

Morana's lips curve as her skin shimmers and her face shifts—her smile stretching into rows of razor-sharp teeth, her nose flattening into a narrow slit, her eyes rising higher and slanting into an inhuman shape.

"Still, if you ever decide to stop running and start fighting—call me." She muses casually as she toes through what's left of the corpses.

Lysander straightens his jacket and nods, his eyes shifting between us and Wren and André outside.

"The kind of chaos you two make? Someone's always in the market for that." He snaps his fingers, and fog begins to coil around us.

"No need to worry about things here," Lysander says, nodding toward the now-entranced humans outside as Wren and André start making their way back to us. "Just try not to draw too much attention from now on."

Then Morana vanishes—no flash, no drama. Just shimmer, then silence. Lysander steps back and moves to meet Wren and André while Liam and I watch.

The slaughterhouse looks like a crime scene—the blood on the floor gleaming like spilled ink. Erin reaches for my hand, our fingers tangling instinctively.

"Ready?" she asks, excitement threading through her voice.

I look past her—beyond the carnage and dust—to the open doors where sunlight spills in.

"With you?" I murmur. "Always."

We step over the wreckage and out into the morning sun. The city waits for us—bright, hungry, and alive. The Elders' curses echo behind us, but neither of us looks back.

Together, hand in hand, we vanish into the early morning light.

CHAPTER TWENTY-ONE

ERIN

Six months ago, I killed our gods.

Or maybe I became one. Hard to tell the difference now.

Tokyo sprawls beneath me like a living circuit board, humming with neon blood and the pulse of a thousand strangers. The air's cool, a breeze tugging at the hem of my jacket as I lounge on the edge of a rooftop no one else could reach. It feels like a secret—the kind of place someone like me can finally breathe. My phone rings in my jacket pocket. I don't need to check the ID—I already know who it is.

I answer with a lazy, "Yes?"

Nathan's voice crackles through the speaker. "Persephone Keres. Always dramatic, aren't we?"

I smirk.

The name still feels fake, but I'm starting to grow into it. "You've got twenty seconds before I hang up."

"News from the ruins. The Elders are scattered. Fae children are refusing alliances. There's blood in the rivers and bodies in the streets. You know—the usual."

"Sounds like peace on Earth."

He chuckles. "You don't miss it? Not even a little?"

I stare out at the skyline, catching the reflection of a paper lantern drifting through the sky.

"Miss it?" I echo. "No. But I haven't forgotten."

A beat.

"There's work in Prague. Something nasty nesting under the opera house. Could use your talents."

"You know where to find me," I say.

"Take care of yourself, Persephone."

I hang up. Behind me, the rooftop door creaks open—and I don't need to look to know it's him.

Liam—Lucien now—walks toward me with two coffee cups and that same stupid little half-smile that makes everything feel real again. His hoodie's up, his steps quiet—but I'd feel him coming miles away. Our bond hums between us.

Still new. Still strange. Still us.

"Everything quiet in the underworld, Persephone?" he teases, passing me a cup.

"Just Nathan playing Oracle," I say, taking a sip.

Black. Scalding. Perfect.

Lucien Keres. My partner in crime. My impossible miracle.

The man who'd died for me—and clawed his way back through death with my blood in his veins. Our names are lies now, chosen from mythology and spite—but our rings are real. I glance down at my left hand, the silver band cool against my skin, engraved on the inside with the words: *"No gods. No masters."'*

His matches mine.

He settles beside me, letting our shoulders press together as he drinks. "I still can't believe you picked 'Persephone.'"

"It suits me," I say, turning to face him. "Queen of the Underworld."

He laughs and bumps my knee with his. "And I'm what—your stealthy husband who probably should've stayed dead?"

I grin. "You're Lucien Keres—supernatural hitman and former Hollywood star. Very tragic. Very handsome."

He pulls up his sleeve and stares at a handwoven bracelet—still stained with blood from that night, still with him. He turns it over in his fingers—a nervous habit he hasn't shaken.

"I miss them," he says suddenly. "My sister. My mom. I know we're not supposed to."

I don't say anything. I just reach into my jacket and touch the locket beneath my shirt. Nathan and Wren's photos still live there, beside my mother's—a reminder of who we are, and what we've bled for.

"I don't miss them," I whisper—meaning the Elders, the cults, the leeches in dark robes who claim power through birthright. "But I miss who we were before all this."

Lucien's hand slides over mine. "We're still those people. Just... now we run things. Now we protect them."

A siren echoes far below. We both look out over the edge of the rooftop, watching the city move around us as if we aren't even here. Ghosts with fake names. Hunters with no gods left to pray to.

"What do you say?" I murmur. "Prague?"

Lucien's eyes gleam. "Only if we burn down the opera house when we're done."

I smile. "Deal."

We stand—two shadows against a flickering skyline—and step off the ledge.

No rules. No thrones.

Just matching rings, shared blood, and the memories we choose to carry. And as we vanish into the night, I feel it again.

That impossible thing neither of us believed in until now.

Hope.

This book exists because of the people who reminded me to keep creating when the world went quiet.

To my husband, Charlie—for your unwavering support, for every meal cooked when I was too lost in a scene, and for believing in this dream before I did.

To my in-laws, who kept the kids laughing when I needed to finish one more chapter—thank you for giving me time to build this world.

To my friends and critique partners, Sean and Marina—your feedback, chaos, and kindness kept this story honest and alive.

To every ARC reader and TikTok follower who took a chance on a debut author: you are the heartbeat of this journey. Thank you for every review, every share, and every late-night message saying you cried, laughed, or saw yourself in these pages.

And to the readers—for letting Erin and Liam's story find you. You are the stars that make this universe shine.

 J. C. Morgan is a Virginia-based author of urban fanta-
sy and supernatural romance. Her stories blend glam-
our, darkness, and emotional depth—exploring what
it means to love in worlds where power and identity
collide.

When she isn't writing, she can be found wrangling her three
boys, experimenting with hair color, or building playlists for her next
book. She lives with her husband, a handful of plants that probably
need watering, and far too many notebooks filled with new story
ideas.

Follow her on TikTok and Instagram @xlilo.of.the.lostx for be-
hind-the-scenes looks at *The Immortal Masquerade* series, and visit
her website at www.jcmorganwrites.com for the latest news on book
releases and merch updates!

Also by J. C. Morgan

The Immortal Masquerade Series
City of Sin (Book 2) – Coming March 2026
Shades of Power (Book 3) – Coming June 2026